# Lilith's
## Awakening

Viktoria Ballavoski

iUniverse, Inc.
Bloomington

# Lilith's Awakening

iUniverse books may be ordered through booksellers or by contacting:

iUniverse
1663 Liberty Drive
Bloomington, IN 47403
www.iuniverse.com
1-800-Authors (1-800-288-4677)

Library of Congress Control Number: 2011918828

ISBN: 978-1-4620-6181-5 (sc)
ISBN: 978-1-4620-6182-2 (hc)
ISBN: 978-1-4620-6183-9 (e)

Printed in the United States of America

iUniverse rev. date: 12/7/2011

# Chapter 1

## *Ruby-Red Skies*

The children were all tucked in their beds; I was set to go to bed myself. I glanced up at the sky. It was crimson, and it had me worried. Last night, I'd witnessed the sky actually turning this crimson red. Was it like the night twenty-six years ago when I gave birth to my twins? I remember my babushka used to say it meant that the demons were out looking for vengeance against the angels. I hoped the next day would be better than today. It had been a busy day. I couldn't get over the poor young woman who came for a session today. There was something about her; as soon as she walked in, I felt the darkness following. I assumed she had come to talk to me, but she asked me to do a Turkish coffee reading instead. As I was telling her that she was being followed by a black shadow, she said anxiously, "We will meet again," and left.

Just as I was about to get into bed, my cell phone rang. It was Detective Michael Benson. He sometimes called me to ask for my services in his unsolved cases.

"Viktoria," he said, "we have a young victim here. I was wondering if you could come and see her. Maybe you can do a cold reading? I feel her presence. By the way, she has your business card in her hand, so you might know her."

"Sure, Michael," I replied. "Give me ten minutes. I'll be right there."

When I arrived, I found Michael right next to the victim. He always seemed to have a serious look on his face. It highlighted his worry lines, which made him seem much older than he really was. And after being in his profession for so long, he even had some gray hairs mixed in with the brown. I did sense the woman's presence; she was still with us, watching over her body, and she was confused. The victim was the woman who had come to see me earlier that day. Her name was Gabriellele. Her large, dark-blue eyes were trying to tell me something; I just didn't realize it at the time.

I proceeded to the victim's body, and just as I was about to touch her, I could hear her speaking in a low tone. "There are six hundred sixty-six of us females to one male. You have to stop Lilith and the others."

I turned around. "What do you mean by that?"

She walked away from me and started to walk into the light, but she was stopped by the black shadow of a woman. It would not allow her to cross through. I was astonished at what I had seen. I could not believe my eyes.

She answered, "I will be back."

*　*　*

That night, when I arrived home, I was still thinking about that mysterious woman. I could not get her out of my mind. I couldn't sleep. I tossed and turned thinking about her for what seemed like hours before I finally fell into an uneasy sleep. As I slept, I could hear Gabriellele repeating, "You have to stop Lilith and the others." I did not know what to make of it.

Though I closed my eyes and managed to sleep, I knew that she was watching me, and I could still hear her. I knew it was Gabriellele. She was there with me. I could feel her sadness but also her warm feelings. I felt the desire to hold her and comfort her and tell her I would be there for her when she needed me.

*I know you are here*, I spoke to her in my thoughts, wondering if she could hear me. *I can sense your presence. Gabriellele, I can sense your energy. You perhaps need to talk to me? I know you are here.*

*What are you frightened of? What have Lilith and her friends done to you? Who are these people? What do they want from you?*

I was trying hard to give her the courage to communicate with me. I knew I had to get her to trust me. The only problem was I did not know how.

The only person who might be able to help me was my husband. He was a psychiatrist; he might have some suggestions as to how I could get her to talk to me, get her to tell me what had happened to her.

I knew he would be upset by what I was about to do, but I needed to wake him up. I went upstairs to our bedroom.

"Brandon, please wake up," I said, giving him a slight shake. "I can't sleep; we have to talk."

"You mean right now?" he asked with a moan. "Can we talk about it at breakfast tomorrow?"

"No, right now," I insisted.

"You've never talked about your cases before. Why now? It's the middle of the night."

"This one is different from the others. This woman came for a reading today. A few hours after she left, I got a call from that detective, Michael. He asked me to meet him at a crime scene. The victim was the same woman! She is here constantly whispering to me, 'Protect them.' I don't know who they are! I don't know where they are! However, she wants me to protect these people."

"Viktoria, try to sleep on it. You've had a long and exhausting day. Maybe you'll be able to communicate with her tomorrow when you have a clearer mind. You might feel better."

"You're probably right," I said with a sigh. "I am worn-out, and I might be overreacting. Good night, honey."

\* \* \*

I woke up the next morning to the smell of brewing coffee. I went to the kitchen to find that Melisa had already left and Lacey and Cameron were set to go to school. Lacey happened to look just like me, except she had her father's blue eyes and blond hair; Cameron and Melisa had my brown hair and green eyes.

"I did not forget, Viktoria," Brandon said as he poured coffee into a travel mug. "We will discuss your situation as soon as I get back from dropping the kids off at school, okay?"

I nodded and gave my kids each a kiss on the cheek as they grabbed their stuff and walked out the door. As soon as they were gone, the phone rang. It was Michael.

"Good morning, Michael. You're up early. You're already at work?"

"Yes, I am. I just called you to tell you about Gabriellele's autopsy results."

"How did you get the results so fast?" I asked as I sat down at the kitchen table, my hot coffee steaming in a mug in front of me.

"The forensics team was so eager that they stayed up all night to determine Gabriellele's cause of death. And they said it was the most uncommon case they had ever seen."

"Tell me," I urged.

"Well, Gabriellele's death was caused by a massive heart attack. Her heart was seriously damaged."

"What's uncommon about a heart attack?"

"Nothing, but, Viktoria, when the medical examiner did the autopsy on the victim, they noticed something that did not make sense. I have never heard of or seen anything like this."

"What was it, Michael?"

"There was not a drop of blood left in the body. Her heart had been torn up somehow, but there were no signs of any bleeding anywhere else."

"How can that be?" I asked, not believing what I was hearing. "How could that happen, Michael?"

"I don't understand it; I don't know how that could have happened, Viktoria, but we need to find out."

"Okay, I'll stop by your office later and try to see what has happened. I'll be in the office in forty minutes. I need to stop by the morgue first."

As I finished talking to the detective, Brandon walked in and said, "I do apologize that we could not discuss this last night. I was too tired to do anything but sleep. But now I'm ready to talk. What were you saying about the victim?" he asked as he pulled out a chair and sat down.

"Last night, Michael called me and asked me to do a cold reading on a victim. When I got there, I discovered that the victim was the same lady who'd come for a reading earlier in the day. Her soul was still there, watching over her body. Speculating and scared, she kept saying, 'You have to rescue them from Lilith.' Gabriellele wants to talk to me, but she is frightened."

"Who is Gabriellele?" he asked, confused.

"Gabriellele is the name of the victim. She kept speaking of six hundred sixty-seven of them and said that I am obligated to protect them from Lilith. I cannot figure it out. Then she said six hundred sixty-six females and one male. What have I got to do with her death?"

"If you're asking me for advice on how to deal with it, I think you should not get involved in this. You're just looking for trouble. The sound of six hundred sixty-six females and one male and this Lilith freaks me out. I have to go now, Viktoria, but if I were you, I would rethink getting involved in this."

"I had better get ready and go; I still need to go see Michael after the morgue."

I felt Gabriellele's presence again. *Gabriellele,* I thought, *I don't know what you're trying to say, what you were involved in. This is a cult, and the leader's name is Lilith? And you want us to save the rest of them from her? Is that it? Is that why you came to see me yesterday? Well, if you don't communicate with me, I can't do much for the others. You know that I'm right. Well, I'm coming over to see you at the morgue. Perhaps you will decide to show yourself to me over there.*

I thought about what Michael had said about the autopsy; the victim's body did not contain a drop of a blood. How could that happen? She had not been shot or stabbed. How did she lose all her blood?

As soon as I got into my car, I noticed my babushka sitting there. "I see you are going to join me to see the victim," I said to my father.

"No, Viktoria, I am here to tell you that you are being watched by jinn. You have to be more cautious; a jinn can form itself into anything. The only way to find out if it's a jinn is by looking into its eyes. The eyes are all black, and the iris is red. Do not look into his or her eyes deeply or show your fears. We are here, remember. I want you to be more cautious when you get to the morgue."

"I am not alone," I said. "I am accompanied by a dark shadow every single step I take."

Later, as I went down the stairs to the morgue, I could feel someone pressing against me, trying to stop me from going any farther. This sensation chilled me to my bones actually. As I got closer, I could smell it, and I became even more frightened; something about the door bothered me. It was open as I was about to walk in, but the doorstop fell away, and the door slammed shut in my face. I could hear the echo thundering up the stairs. *Clearly,* I thought, *you should not be here.*

I knew someone or something was trying to scare me, but I was going to do what I needed to. I said to whatever it was, "You will not frighten or stop me." As I was about to walk in, it warned me again not to go any closer to Gabriellele.

"Oh, my lord! Are you all right?" asked Dr. James, Stainfield the medical examiner. "How did that door slam on you the way it did? The doorstopper fell; did you see that?"

"Yes, I did, and I am okay. I'm just fine. My name is Viktoria Nelson. I'm the medium for this case."

"Yes, I know, Michael told me you would be stopping by. I just finished wrapping up. Gabriellele was the most popular victim today.

She was accompanied by a few priests, who carried out an unusual exorcism over here."

"Why would they do it over here? Couldn't they take her to the church and do it there?"

"One of the priests mentioned something about an evil soul. I was not such a big believer, but after what I saw, I do respect her family's request for it before they take her to the funeral home."

"What did you see, Dr. James?"

"You should have been here and seen it with your own eyes. It was an incredible thing that happened. Something black and thick came out of her mouth! It was unbelievable! I thought I was watching a scary movie. Then the priest baptized her by spraying her with some holy water. It was an exciting and interesting day for Gabriellele and me."

"That would make sense," I said, referring to the holy water. "Otherwise, they would not be able to take her inside the church."

"Furthermore, there was a woman who came by as well. There was something about that woman. She waited outside while the priests did the exorcism. Soon after they left, she kept coming to look at Gabriellele but from far away and with hate in her eyes, I dare say. When I asked her for her name, she said it was Lily. I asked her if she was related to the victim. She just looked at me with her deep black eyes, but her pupils were red! She did not say anything else." After a moment of silence, he continued, "You have a few minutes before they pick her up."

"Okay. I won't be long. Thanks."

I approached the body. It did not look like Gabriellele's. This was a totally different body. I was stunned.

"Dr. James!" I called out to him, keeping my eyes on the body. "Is this Gabriellele's body?"

"Yes, Viktoria. This is the only body brought in last night. Her name is on the tag."

"That might be, but this does not look like the woman who came to my house and whom I saw at the crime scene. This body looks older and has burn spots."

"It's the holy water. It burns, the priest said. I asked him the same question."

"I know there is something you have to tell me, Gabriellele," I whispered to the body. "Please, let's talk about it. What I am seeing now does not make any sense. I do not recognize this body, Gabriellele. I am over here to help you. Who are the rest of the six hundred sixty-six of them? How can I help them?"

I could hear her saying repeatedly, "They need to be saved from Lilith and the others." She then said, "Please go away from here! Now you are in danger! Go now! I will find you. We will talk about it later."

"Okay. Gabriellele, I'm leaving, but I will be waiting for your signs. Together, we will save them from whatever it is."

"Viktoria," Dr. James said, as he moved closer to me, "are you done? The family's here to take her."

"Yes, I'm finished. Thanks. See you later, Dr. James."

Gabriellele was their only child; I felt for the family. I offered my condolences to them. I didn't know what I would do if I were in their situation. I did not even want to imagine it. My prayers were with the family. I wouldn't wish this on my worst enemy.

By this time, I just wanted to go home, hug my kids, tell them how much I loved them, and ask God to bless them. I thanked God with every breath they took and hoped that he might watch over them.

Gabriellele's family did not want to give her a big funeral, and they wanted to bury her the same day.

A few hours later, I went to the funeral to pay my respects. I was hoping to see Gabriellele lying in the open casket. I approached the coffin carefully and looked at her. What I saw did not look like her. They had her dressed up so an angel could not take his eyes off of her, but she still did not look like the lady who had come to my house for a reading and whose body I later saw at the crime scene. There were additional burn spots on her. Even though the makeup artist tried to cover them up, I could still see them.

I needed to talk to Michael. He might have seen her before the priest sprinkled holy water on her. I walked away in shock. How could this happen? I just could not wait to find out. As soon as I found an opportunity, I sat down next to Gabriellele's mother, wondering what sort of explanation I would get. Unfortunately, I felt the sorrow and could not, in good conscience, ask her any questions.

I decided to go with them to the burial site. The priest started the ceremony with a prayer and then sprinkled the holy water. When I was able to, I stood next to the grave and noticed that it was deeper than normal and the coffin had double locks.

*What is going on here?* I wondered.

The ceremony ended, and we all walked away from the grave site. I had lots of questions in my head but no answers.

I looked at Gabriellele's mother, Mrs. Cecil (I had finally learned her last name from the medical examiner). She looked confused, hurt, and angry. I walked up beside her and introduced myself. She was surprised to see me there.

"What does a psychic have to do with this case?" she asked.

"Mrs. Cecil, I am a medium. I am able to see and talk to the dead. I work with the police to solve unusual cases like Gabriellele's. Mrs. Cecil, I know it is not the right time for any kind of questions, but may I ask you something?"

"Of course you can," she said with concern. "I will try to answer whatever you need."

"Who is Lilith? Did Gabriellele ever mention her to you or anyone else? Do you know if she was involved in some sort of cult?"

"You mean Gabriellele has spoken to you?"

"Yes, Gabriellele keeps telling me to save them from Lilith and the others. Mrs. Cecil, the first time I saw Gabriellele was at the investigation. Did she look different to you? She looked different to me, and I was wondering why that is?"

"We adopted Gabriellele. When she was few a days old, her

birth mother passed away. We never baptized her. We're not really Christian. When we took her to the church for the funeral, the priest suggested that it would be a good idea to baptize her. We agreed with the priest."

"What about the burns?"

"The priest said Gabriellele's body had been taken over by a demon, and he had to do an exorcism. Only then would they baptize her, and afterward, she could rest in peace. The burns are from a reaction to the holy water. I believe they also said she had been bitten by a vampire demon, which would explain why her blood was gone."

"I don't know much about vampires, Mrs. Cecil. The police have not mentioned anything to me about a vampire biting her. If I hear anything, I will inform you right away."

"Thank you, Viktoria. I would appreciate that."

"Thank you so much again, Mrs. Cecil. You have to be strong. My prayers are with you and your family."

"Viktoria, is my Gabriellele here now? If she is, can you tell her we loved her, as if she really was our own?"

"Yes, Mrs. Cecil, she is here. You can tell her whatever you need to; I'm sure she would be very happy to hear that from you."

"Gabriellele, we loved you so much. We always will. Can you ever forgive us for not being better parents to you? We would have liked to have been."

I listened for a moment as Gabriellele spoke to me. "Mrs. Cecil, Gabriellele says that you were the best parents anyone could have had, and she loved you and her father very much. And she thanks you."

"Thank you, Viktoria, for giving me this last chance to talk to my baby, to express my feelings to her, and to say my farewell."

"That's okay, Mrs. Cecil. If it's okay with you, can I stop by very soon? To discuss Gabriellele, her friends, and what she would have been doing in her spare time?"

"Of course, any night, dear." I gave her a hug and told her it was from her little girl. Then I walked away.

I do not know why I got so emotionally involved with that case. Something was pulling me. I was desperately searching for answers.

It had been a long day. I needed to stop at the office and drop off the report from Michael. Just as I was thinking this, my phone rang.

"Michael," I said when I answered it, "I was thinking of stopping by and dropping off the report, but can I give it to you tomorrow?"

"How was the funeral ceremony?" he asked instead of answering my question.

"It was a strange but interesting ceremony. I spoke to Mrs. Cecil; she seemed like a very loving and caring mother. She looked lost and devastated by Gabriellele's death. As a mother, I understand; she was the only child she had. Did you know Gabriellele was adopted when she was only a few days old?"

"No, I did not know that. It must be a horrible experience, losing a child. That is beyond my imagination." He sighed. "I will see you tomorrow."

I walked into the house and went straight to Lacey and Melisa, gave them a hug, and held on; I did not want to leave. As a parent, I could not imagine burying my child.

\* \* \*

A few days later, while I was on the phone with Michael, I got a call from Mrs. Cecil.

"Have to cut this short, Michael. I have Mrs. Cecil on the other line. I hope she has remembered something." I switched over to the other line. "Hi, Mrs. Cecil. Is everything okay?"

"Yes, it is. We need to talk about Gabby and her friend Lilith and her ritual."

"Who is Gabby, Mrs. Cecil?" I asked, confused.

"It's Gabriellele. I used to call her Gabby. Her biological mother's last wish was for us to call her Gabby. I am sorry if I have confused you."

"That's okay. I will come by tomorrow."

"No, I need to talk to you immediately; it's important. I have to show you other things concerning this matter."

"What about if I sent a detective over? He is in charge of this case, and he needs all the information he can get."

"No, that won't work. I really need to talk to you and no one else. It will only take a few minutes of your time."

"Mrs. Cecil, I really would like it if Michael came with me. I don't usually go without a detective, and Michael is important in this case."

"I don't want to discuss this with anyone besides you because it is personal, and privacy is important to me and her father. We can only talk to you. Perhaps you might help us to understand what she used to practice."

"All right then. Let me call the station and let them know I will be late." I dialed Michael's number on my phone. "Hi, Michael, I'm going over to see Mrs. Cecil. She wants to talk to me, and it has to be today. When I told her I would be happier if you could join us, she said no and insisted that I be alone."

"Okay, but be careful. Call me when you get there, or if you need me."

"Okay. Michael, can you do me a favor? Call Brandon and let him know I might be late. I tried but he wasn't picking up his phone."

"Yes, I'll call him and let him know."

"Oh my Lord, Gabriellele," I said as I walked to the car. "I'm so glad you're here. I'm going over to see your mom. She has something to tell me. She also mentioned that you have been practicing a ritual. I'm surprised—"

Before I could say any more, she cut me off. "Viktoria, do not go over there. It's a setup! Listen, Viktoria, you will get hurt. Don't go! I don't think it was my mom who called you. It's a setup!"

"Gabriellele," I reasoned, "it has to be your mom. I have given my number to no one besides your mom! And she sounded sincere. I need some sort of answer; she might know something. Anyway, I'm not going alone. You are here. I can also feel the presence of my mom and dad, my guardian angels."

"Whatever you do, do not go into that house; that house is hell! Please go back! It's Lilith doing this. She must have found out that my soul is still here with you, and she does not want us to mess up her plans! She can be so convincing. Trust me, you should not go!"

"Gabriellele, I cannot turn back. I think you're overreacting. Really, who is Lilith? How can she impersonate your mother? I'm not turning back now; I'm almost there."

"Okay, go. But you must stay outside. Do not go in! It is an evil place! Stay outside even if she gets extremely persistent!"

"Fine, I will not go inside."

"Viktoria, I will watch you closely, but I cannot go in, nor can your father. If we do, they will pull us down to the vortex that takes us to hell where there are demons!"

"You mean Lilith, Adam's first wife and the mother of the demons? Is that what you were trying to tell me?"

"Yes, Viktoria! Lilith and the others are up to something! Please be careful!"

I didn't want to say anything, but I had a premonition of the vortex as I got closer to the house. My heart started beating faster, and cold sweat dripped down my face. Maybe I should have listened to Gabriellele. However, I didn't want to give up. I had to help her and the others.

When I went up to the porch, I called out, "Mrs. Cecil, are you there? It's Viktoria."

"Come in! The door is open, Viktoria," Mrs. Cecil replied.

"Mrs. Cecil, it's getting late. Besides, I've left the car running. Perhaps you can bring the files outside."

"There is some stuff I cannot bring outside."

"No, Mrs. Cecil, I can't stay too long. I have to drive back. Let's talk on the porch. What is it you wanted to talk about?"

"All right, dear, but this will not take long. Come on in." She came outside, and we sat on the chairs, which faced the street. "Viktoria, what I am about to tell you, you cannot repeat to anyone."

"Why? I have to report to my superior; I can't hide anything."

"You have to back away from this case. It's dangerous. You and your family will get hurt."

"What do you mean by 'back away'? Are you threatening me or warning me, Mrs. Cecil?"

"Don't get me wrong, dear; I am only having this conversation with you because I have something to show you. It's where she practiced her evil, demonic stuff. Come inside."

"Don't go inside!" Gabriellele warned me. "There is no such place! I never practiced anything! She is trying to take you to the vortex!"

*Okay, calm down, Gabriellele,* I thought. I asked Mrs. Cecil, "What are you talking about, Mrs. Cecil? Nothing about Gabriellele's death was normal. Her autopsy shows her main arteries were ripped out; her heart was crushed, and much of it was damaged. This can only happen if a person has a traumatic impact injury, like from falling from the twentieth floor or being hit by a bus. We all know that her body was found on the sidewalk. She was not hit by a car, nor did she fall from the twentieth floor. There was not a bruise or broken bone in her body. How she really died is the question."

I did not listen to Gabriellele and went inside. I felt extremely unwelcome, and I saw Gabriellele watching from the window. She was yelling, "Viktoria! Come out from there! You are in danger!"

"Come into the dining room, Viktoria. I have the document over here by the desk."

# Chapter 2

## Face-to-Face

When I walked into the dining room, I felt a kind of coldness. There was also a unique and horrible smell. It had the aroma of burned flesh mixed with an odd, musky scent. Suddenly, I heard Gabriellele rush inside. She was trying to save me, knowing she could be dragged into the hell.

"Viktoria, get out! There is a demon and trap hole right in front of you! Don't take another step!"

I tried to move away, but something held me back. It was my dad, trying to hold me so I would not fall into the vortex. A black mist thrust itself at me. I knew it was the demon; I desperately tried to spray him with the holy water and throw some salt at him while praying verses I knew.

Unfortunately, I did not get a chance to do any of those things. The demon blew more of the black mist. The wind threw me off. It was so powerful that I lost my balance and fell into the hole. I could hear my dad telling me to stay calm and try to fight back. As I tried to make my way up again, the demon, with great strength, blew me back into the hole.

This situation was getting out of control! Hell was pulling me; it was too hard to control. I could not ask for help from Gabriellele. "Mrs. Cecil's already trapped her," Babushka was telling me. "Try to calm down. I am holding you. Do not fight back!"

Three angels appeared. I could not see their faces, but the energy they gave me provided the help I needed to get out of that hole.

*   *   *

The next thing I remember is waking up in a hospital with a concussion, some broken ribs, and Mrs. Cecil beside my bed.

"What has happened, Mrs. Cecil?" I moaned.

"I don't know. When I got home, I found you on my front lawn."

"What do you mean when you got home? I remember that you were in the dining room, and you asked me to come in. You had some documents to show me, so I walked in. There was a hole that I fell into. I think Gabriellele was right. She told me that we were being set up by Lilith; she was disguised as you and holding back Gabriellele. Gabriellele told me that it was a setup, but I just ignored her."

"Dear," Mrs. Cecil said softly as she patted my arm, "I was not home. I got a message from you that you wanted to meet me at Barb's Café. I waited for you for about an hour. I called you, but you did not answer your phone, so decided to come home. I do not know anything about the documents. I found you on my front lawn. I was surprised to see you there since you were supposed to meet me at the café."

"Mrs. Cecil, I never sent you messages," I said nervously. "It was all Lilith's doing, not mine!"

"Yes, you did," she insisted. "I was supposed to meet you there. You gave me the address. Here's my phone; your message should still be there."

"Mrs. Cecil, I received a call from you. You said you had something important to talk to me about. I was inside your house talking to you. You even told me to stay out of this case and not to tell anyone what we had discussed. But now that I know that it was not you, I know for fact that neither of us called the other. You were talking to Lilith. She set us up."

"I may be old, but I have an excellent memory. I was not there. And there are no documents to show you."

"I know, Mrs. Cecil. I realize that it was not you. Lilith disguised herself as both of us so that I would back off from this case."

"Okay then. Let me get this straight—I did not call you, and you didn't call me? Then who did?"

"I told you, Mrs. Cecil, it was Lilith who set us up. She is trying to stop me from finding out about whatever it is Gabriellele warned me about. She even said it was a setup, and it was Lilith and the others." Just at that moment, Brandon walked in. "Brandon, how did you know I was here?"

"Michael called."

"Who called Michael?"

"Mrs. Cecil called when she found you."

"Yes, dear. I checked your last call; I redialed the number."

"Thank you, Mrs. Cecil."

"Dear, you don't have to thank me; I'm pleased to see that you're okay. When I found you, I got so scared! I didn't know what had happened."

"Don't worry, Mrs. Cecil. We'll find out what is going on. I promise you, and we will end this nonsense," I said.

"Viktoria, how could you go into a place like that? Why didn't you ask Michael to go with you?"

"Well, I feel much better, Brandon," I said, ignoring his questions. "Can you take me home?"

"While you talk, I'll talk to the doctor about getting you signed out—"

Just at that moment, Dr. Francis walked in. "I can't sign the release yet. You're under twenty-four-hour observation."

I was about to argue when I heard Gabriellele telling me I should listen to her and stay in the hospital at least one night.

This time, I decided to listen to Gabriellele, and I stayed.

Once everyone had left, it was so quiet that I started thinking about my children and wondering how they were doing. I was amazed how deeply I missed them already.

"Gabriellele, I know you're here," I said to the air. "And I do thank you for warning me. We have to talk about what has been going on. If you want help, you have to start communicating; I need to know everything that you know. How did this happen? What is up with Lilith? No more beating around the bush! I need answers, because whatever this is almost got me killed! I think I am entitled to an explanation sooner or later."

"Viktoria," I heard Gabriellele say in response, "I told you not to go into the house. I told you it was a setup and you did not listen. Don't worry; I'm going to tell you everything, but not right at this moment. You have to relax and get back on your feet."

"You know what, Gabriellele? This all started after you came for a reading. That night, the sky was red. My dad always said that when the sky turned red, the doors to hell opened. This must be Lilith; I know a few people who know about her but not many. However, I hope to find out about her and her demons or jinns. I will get the answers from Greg; he will update me.

"Gabriellele, now I know what you were trying to say, but don't worry. We'll find out what is going on and stop them from doing whatever they are trying to do."

"Viktoria, try to relax and get some rest, and we will talk about this later."

All of a sudden, I had a premonition. This one was of Lacey calling me.

"Mom?" Lacey asked, panic woven into her voice. "Can you hear me? There is something unknown in our house! I cannot see it, but I feel it!"

"Lacey," I said out loud, knowing she could hear me, "I can hear you, baby. Don't worry. I will be there soon. For now, pretend you are sleeping. Don't leave your room, and keep on praying."

"Okay, Mom," she whispered in reply.

Demons had entered my house and were watching my children.

I needed to find out who was there. Why were they there? I was just hoping they wouldn't hurt them. I did not want to call and panic them. "Gabriellele, I have to go over there through an out-of-body experience, and I want you to come with me."

"Might as well. I'll come with you. But before that, do you want me to go there and see if it is safe for you to enter?"

"Perhaps that would be better, Gabriellele. Just be careful. Don't let them see you."

\*　\*　\*

It was getting late; I was starting to worry. What was taking Gabriellele so long? I just hoped everything was fine; she should have been back by then.

"Viktoria," Gabriellele said when she finally returned, "I'm back now, so you can go. It's not that safe though. There is a jinn in the house! I did not go into your house, so they didn't see me. I didn't want them to get mad, so I watched them from outside. Everyone is in their room sleeping. Should be fine as long as we do not aggravate them or let them see us."

"Before that though, I need to put the cross on, spray holy water on myself, and make a circle with salt for my protection."

"Why holy water and salt?"

"Because I don't want evil spirits to obtain my body. We don't have time to waste, so let's go."

It took me a long time to get everything set up. I didn't know what was wrong; this had never happened before. I couldn't seem to concentrate. I was so scared that a demon would hurt my family or take over my body that I couldn't grasp what I was doing. Finally, I cleared my mind and was spiritually at my home checking on the kids. I noticed all the religious symbols we had hanging around had been turned upside down.

When I went into my bedroom, I saw two demon warriors standing there, guarding Brandon. It was strange. Why would they want him? I was scared that they might hurt him, but I had to get closer. As I neared him, Brandon shouted, "Lilith!" He didn't sound so much scared as he did frustrated. I heard him saying that he had made a bad choice and that he had been praying since then. *What in God's name is he talking about?* I wondered.

"Oh, God," he moaned. "They know we're here."

"Gabriellele, we have to go right now," I insisted.

"Viktoria, you go ahead. Make sure they don't follow you. I will confuse them. Go now, Viktoria! They are coming after you. I don't want them to follow us."

As Gabriellele kept them focused on her, I went back into my body. I hoped that I had not been followed by any of them. I don't think I had been. I wondered how Gabriellele was doing. I hoped they did not recognize her; if they did, they would capture her and take her to hell using whatever force necessary.

"Viktoria, I'm here, and I'm fine," Gabriellele said from the side of my bed. "Don't worry about me."

"Start talking. What the hell is happening, Gabriellele? How is my husband involved with Lilith? I could hear him calling out her name! What is he doing with these evil spirits? I know for fact he does not practice any kind of black magic or rituals. I cannot deal with this by myself, Gabriellele. Do you know Brandon or anything about him?"

"No, I don't know anything about him, and that is the truth. I only know about Lilith. She is the reason for my birth as well as my death."

"As soon as I get out of here, I'm going to consult my friend, who is a demonologist."

"Please, Viktoria, do not involve another person. That will only make matters worse. Together, we can do it, and you have the power."

"Don't worry. I am not going to involve anyone else … yet … unless I need to. But I have to find out what I am actually dealing with; I'm just inquiring about it. My biggest question is why are Lilith's warriors guarding Brandon?" I sighed as I looked at the time. "It's late. You can hang around if you want to, but I need a good rest."

All night long, I tossed and turned. I could not wait until the next day when Brandon could get me out of there. I decided not to tell anyone about what I had seen the night before. He was already complaining that I was putting the family in danger. I'd always disagreed with him up to the present moment.

It was eight thirty in the morning. I had to call Greg before Brandon got there. A nurse walked into my room. What got me were her eyes. They were almost all black, but even the whites creeped me out. She wanted to give me medicine, but I refused to take it. She was persistent, saying I should take the medicine; it was the doctor's orders. There was something about her that made me really uncomfortable, but I did not want to argue with her, so I pretended to place the pill in my mouth, but I kept it under my tongue.

As she was walking out of the room, another nurse, named Judy, walked in. She asked, "Are you new? I've never seen you." The other nurse just looked at her with a nasty smirk and walked away without saying anything.

"That's strange," Nurse Judy said before coming over to the bed and looking at my file. "Never seen her before, and no one has said anything about a new nurse coming in. Viktoria, was she here all night?"

"I don't think so. I did see her last night; there was another nurse who came in. I think her name is Rosemary."

"Did the nurse mention her name to you? Why was she in your room?"

"No, she didn't say anything about her name. She was here to give me medicine; she said that it was the doctor's orders and I had to take it."

"Do you know what the medicine looked like?"

"I have it here. I did not feel comfortable taking it. I pretended that I did but hid it under my tongue. Here it is." I opened my palm to show her the small pink pill.

"Give it to me, Viktoria; I need to see what kind of medicine it is, because you were not supposed to take any medicine at all. You have a few more tests to do. Thank God you did not take it."

"You can say that again. What kind of medicine is it?"

"I don't know, but I'll find out and let you know. I've never seen this medicine before, Viktoria. I'll see you later."

I was desperate to call Greg as soon as possible before anything else happened. I thought I might need his protection as well.

I reached across my bed to get the phone on the stand. I dialed the number and waited for him to pick up. "Good morning, Greg," I said in answer to his "Hello?" "I know it's early, but I had no choice; I need to see you as soon as possible."

"Good morning, Viktoria. That's okay. I've been waiting for your call. What is it? Hold on one second; who is next to you? I believe you have someone else there. I can feel the harmful energy around you."

"No one except Gabriellele, Greg," I said. "It's a long story; I'll tell you everything when I see you at the café this afternoon. About one o'clock? Is that good for you?"

"That's fine with me. Be careful, Viktoria; you're being followed by a harmful energy."

"I will be careful. I'll see you later."

As soon as I hung up, Brandon walked in. "You're up early this morning," I noted before he gave me a kiss on the lips. As he settled in next to me on the bed, I asked, "You couldn't sleep either?"

"I took the kids to school and then came over here. The kids and I miss you. All night, Cameron kept asking for you. You know how he gets when he doesn't see you home. He bombards us with questions."

"That's my boy," I said with a smile. "He is the most sensitive child I have ever seen." I took a deep breath and changed the subject. "I was told that they have more tests to run. I just want to go home."

"Don't rush, Viktoria. Dr Francis is not in yet; we have to wait for her. By the way, how do you feel?"

"I'm much better. I'm glad I stayed over, though. I was knocked out."

"I got breakfast for you," he said and then held up a bag. It smelled delicious. "Thought you might be hungry."

"Yes, I am. Starving, in fact, but they said I can't eat anything. However, they didn't say anything about not having anything to drink so I am assuming I can have coffee at least. Pass that to me please. I really need it."

He reached into the bag and took out a cup. "Michael called me up this morning and said you should stay out a couple of days and rest. He also offered to get someone to pick up the kids from school."

I took a sip of the much-needed coffee. "That's nice of him. I'm sure Cameron would love to be picked up by a police car. I don't know about Lacey; she might complain about it. It's an early dismissal today too. But he does not have to do that; I'm fine. I need to go out anyway. I have errands to run."

"All right then, but at least let the police pick up the kids. Don't overdo it." He looked out the open door. "Let me see if the doctor is here." As he went to the doorway, Dr. Francis walked in. "Good morning, Dr. Francis. I was coming over to see you."

Dr. Francis walked up to the bed. "How is the patient doing today? You should be able to go home as soon as we take you to get an MRI just to make sure everything is okay."

"Why an MRI? I'm fine, Dr. Francis."

"Just to be sure. We need to do it. Better safe than sorry. Someone should be here shortly to take you. It won't take long. By the way, Viktoria, Nurse Judy showed me the tablet. I'm glad you didn't take it, or we would be trying to save your life right now."

"What did you say? What would it have done?"

"Well, it was a radiation tablet. We usually give them to cancer patients. The nurse accidentally gave them to you. I suppose it was for the patient next door. We give her only one once a week; I don't know how someone could make a mistake like that," she said with a shake of her head. "No one has seen her before, and we haven't seen her again."

"Thank the Lord!"

"Viktoria, what's gone on?" Brandon asked, worried. "Why didn't you tell me about this earlier? I have a right to know about it! I would never forgive myself if anything happened to you; I should have stayed here last night."

"You may be right. I'm sorry, Brandon, I should have told you. But I didn't want you to worry, and besides, nothing happened. I'm fine!"

"If the patient is ready, we could take her to the MRI," Dr. Francis said.

"I'm coming too," Brandon said, as he took my hand. "I won't let you go by yourself; I need to be there with you."

"Don't worry, Brandon," I said, putting my hand over his and patting it. "You're overreacting."

"I will be there, Brandon, at all times," Dr. Francis assured him. "I will keep an eye on her, believe me. She is under my care from now on; I give you my word."

"Thanks, Dr. Francis. I believe you."

Just as they were about to wheel me away, I thought of something. "I don't think I can stay forty-five minutes in that MRI machine; I am close to claustrophobic. I don't think I would be able to sit in there for long."

"Don't worry, Viktoria; it's comfortable. If you think there's a problem, let us know, and we will pull you out."

"Gabriellele, are you still here?" I whispered, hoping Dr. Francis couldn't hear me.

"Yes, Viktoria, I'm here. I think they did follow us last night, but don't worry, it's safe … for now."

"All right then. As soon as I am out of here, we're going to see Greg."

"Did you say something, Viktoria?" Dr. Francis asked me.

"No, just talking to myself," I said weakly.

I went into the machine and closed my eyes. I prayed that I would not panic. Before I knew it, the doctor was saying, "It's all done, Viktoria. You see how easy it was? Soon, we'll take you to your room, and then you can go home. I want to see you in two days to go over the results and give you a checkup, understand?"

I nodded. She wheeled me back to my room, where I saw Gabriellele watching me. "You see?" I said, once the doctor was gone. "Nothing happened, I'm fine. The MRI was not as bad as I thought it would be. I just want to get dressed and get out of here as soon as possible."

"Are you still going to see Greg?" she asked as I changed in the bathroom. "What if he is one of them? There are a lot of people involved in this matter; psychics … people in government, hospitals, schools, restaurants—they're everywhere! I'm afraid, Viktoria, after what happened today, and you should be too."

I came out of the bathroom and put my hospital gown on the bed. "No, I am not afraid. I believe that I deserve some sort of explanation. As soon as I get home, I will make an excuse to leave the house for a short time. I told you, Gabriellele, I cannot wait to see Greg. Let's see what explanation he has for me."

* * *

At last, home sweet home, but since the night before, the house looked different to me. I thought I was still under the influence of what happened then.

"Hi, kids, I'm home!" I yelled out. I could hear Melisa, Lacey, and Cameron running down the stairs. "Oh God!" I said with much joy as I wrapped my arms around them. "It's so good to hear your voices! I missed you all and love you all so much!"

"Viktoria," Brandon said. It surprised me since I did not think he would be home. "If anyone heard you talking like this, they might think you had been a way for years, not overnight." He came closer to me and gave me a hug. "Welcome home, honey. It did feel as long as a year without you."

As much as I loved seeing Brandon, I couldn't understand why he would be home. As I pulled back, I asked him, "Brandon, aren't you supposed to be at work? Go ahead. I'm fine. Don't worry, the kids are here."

He refused at first, but after much persuasion, he agreed. Before he left, though, he made sure the kids understood what they needed to do and reminded them to call him if any kind of emergency came up. Then he left.

Lacey came to stand next to me. She was very sensitive but did not like to show any affection. I was surprised when she hugged me and told me how much she had missed me even though I'd been gone only for one night. Suddenly, out of nowhere, she asked, "Who is that woman next to you, Mom?"

That was when I realized she could see Gabriellele. "Do you see her?"

"Yes, Mom. I realize that Cameron and Melisa do not, but she's been next to you since you came in. No one said anything, but last night, I saw her. She was watching us through the window."

"Her name is Gabriellele. We'll talk about this later." To the rest of the group, I said, "Come on, let's go upstairs. I need a shower, and you kids need to finish your homework. Then later tonight, we can go out and celebrate Mommy's homecoming."

"Can I have an ice cream?" Cameron asked hopefully.

"Of course," I said as I lightly touched the top of his head. "You can have as much as you want."

"Love you, Mom!"

I smiled as I said, "However, you have to hurry up and finish your homework!"

They ran upstairs and went into their respective rooms. As I got closer to my room, I hesitated to go in. I felt the coldness from last night again. Lilith really had been in my room, but why?

"What's wrong, Mom?" Lacey asked as she came out of her room holding an empty cup. "Why don't you go in?"

I didn't want to scare her, so I lied. "I thought I heard something, but it was … it was nothing, Lacey."

"Is it about last night, Mom?" she asked as she came closer to me. "I know you were here with Gabriellele; I heard you. I didn't come out of my room, as you told me, but I saw her. I don't know why, but recently, I've been having a premonition. The day you got sick, I felt like I had I been seeing and hearing things, and I did not know what was happening. I was so frightened! Then Grandma, she explained it to me—"

I cut her off. I was surprised. "You see Grandma? Since when, Lacey?"

"I've seen her since she passed away a few years ago. We talk after everyone has gone to bed. She said she and Babushka are watching over the family, and she also said, 'Don't be afraid.' She said I have something special, and I should use it wisely, but only when it is needed. Whenever we need one of them, she told me to just chant her name or Babushka's and they will be with us."

"Lacey, honey, I know you are going through changes, and we will talk about it tonight, but right now, I need to go to Uncle Greg's. I want you to take care of your brother. If your dad calls, tell him I went to pick up a prescription; don't mention anything about Uncle Greg, understand?"

"Why don't you want Dad to know that you're going to see Uncle Greg? Mom, I'm scared something is going to happen to you. Can you please stay?"

"He won't understand, sweetie. We'll tell him later. He'll stop me from going over there after what just happened."

As usual, Cameron came in complaining he was hungry. "Mom, can we order a pizza?"

Sighing, I said, "Okay, go ahead. Order pizza." I turned back to my daughter. "I need to leave now, Lacey."

"Is Gabriellele coming with you?" she asked me.

"Yes, she is. Why?"

She shrugged. "I just don't want you to go anywhere alone. Please call us."

"All right, Lacey. Please, I don't want you to worry about me. I will be just fine."

As I was driving away, I saw Brandon coming. I panicked. I didn't know what to do.

He came up to the car. "You look like you've seen a ghost," he joked. "Where are you going?"

"Just running errands. I need to pick up a prescription. Then I will stop by the store to get some ice cream and coffee."

"Why didn't you give it to me before I left? I would have dropped it off at the pharmacy and picked it up for you later."

"I totally forgot about it when you left. Thanks anyway, honey. I won't be long; I'll be back in a jiffy."

"Viktoria, do you really need to go? I will get it for you."

"Baby, it's okay. I need fresh air; it may do me some good. Also, I might stop by a nail salon and get a manicure, so don't worry. I'll be fine. Trust me. By the way, can you pick up Grandma Nelly; we are going out for dinner."

"Okay, then I'll see you later. Call me if you need me."

*Thank God*, I thought as I saw him walk away. I thought he was going to tag along with me.

I took my phone out of my purse and dialed a number. "Hi, Greg, I'm on my way. I know I'm late, but I will be there in a few minutes. Go ahead, order some coffee and a double espresso for me." When I hung up, I turned to Gabriellele. "Stay with me. Greg is a very nice person. I know you can't trust everyone, but he's okay."

"I don't want anything to go wrong, Viktoria. I will be here."

When I arrived, I pulled into a spot and started looking for him. "There he is." We walked over to his table, and when he saw us, he stood up. I shook his hand. "It is so good to see you, Greg."

"Viktoria, I see you have been followed," he noted, looking past me.

"You're joking, right? As far as I know, only Gabriellele is with us." I looked around the café. "Greg, I see another one right next to the tree. She's watching us. Do you think she has realized we can see her?"

I turned to Gabriellele. "Gabriellele, do you think you can get close and observe her? She's standing farthest away, watching us. You might know who she is."

"Viktoria, I have seen her before, but I don't know where ... Oh! Now I know who it is! It's the nurse from the hospital! The one who gave you the wrong tablet! She vanished into nowhere."

"What's going on?" I wondered. "Can you follow her, Gabriellele?"

"I don't think so. She's already gone."

"What's going on?" Greg echoed me. "Viktoria, is that the one who has been giving you that negative energy I was asking you about this morning?"

"I think so, Greg. I don't know what's going on, but I need your help. You're the only person who can help me."

As we sat down, he said, "Viktoria, these people are called jinns, which is another word for some kind of demons. The jinn is said to be a creature with free will made of smokeless fire by God. They are also known as divinities of inferior status, having many human idiosyncrasies. From time to time, they appear as human creatures, but they are accompanying her, Lilith. Lilith is the first wife of Adam. When she refused to obey and return to Adam, Lilith became a lover of demons, turned against God, and produced hundreds of babies a day. God sent three angels to order her to go back to Adam, but she refused to do so because she said she would not be beneath Adam. Lilith chose Lucifer. God ordered the angels to take her demon children away from her if she did not return to Adam. When the angels took her demon babies away from her, she sought revenge by harming newborns, mostly boys, and to get back at God, she promised herself no man should be greater than she and the rest of the women.

"There are believers that say one day Lilith will keep her word, and she did as well. She decided to use jinns, who by taking their partner's place, got six hundred sixty-six woman pregnant. They had all girl demon babies. She will give them the power to open all the doors to hell.

"Therefore, she thought it was time to keep her promise for revenge, and she has used Lucifer. He joined forces with her to open the doors to hell. It was the only way to do it. Lilith seduces the men, while the jinn appear as their women's partners or husbands. He then seduces and gets the woman pregnant.

"They have been doing this all over the world and have six hundred sixty-six female jinns. However, there was a set of twins that a former worshiper selfishly agreed to sacrifice for success and power, without realizing the babies' father was Lucifer. He switched places with the actual father one night while he was working late, and the twins were conceived. The father realized he could not go through with sacrificing the babies, and he begged for forgiveness and prayed for help from God and the angels. Leila, the angel of birth, heard him, and she knew he was genuine. In exchange, he told Leila everything. He knew about Lilith and what she planned to do with all the children born at the same time. Together, they had power. Female demons have the power to demolish the entire face of the earth. Lilith had never considered twins; one could be a male, and the biological father would be Lucifer. That male born would have been six hundred sixty-seven.

"When the worshiper's wife became pregnant by Lucifer and the other baby was a male, Lilith was furious because she knew Lucifer's son would have the upper hand on everything, especially when it came to the powers, which she did not want. She was trying to get back at God. Lilith has also been trying to get rid of Lucifer and his demon army, but the male born would have to be on Lucifer's side; that would make Lucifer more powerful. Then she would not be able to rule hell with all her female demons. Lilith had no choice but to command the death of the demons. Fortunately, Leila, the angel of birth, saved the male twins during the birth. However, there was another male baby that was stillborn. Leila switched babies. Lilith did want to see the body of a male twin demon. Therefore, the death demon took the baby's body back to Lilith. Leila and another angel, Quelamia, joined forces and gave the twins powers. Together, they have the power to close the door forever.

"Twenty-seven years later, Lilith decided it was time for all the forces to join with the rest of the female demons and come out to start doomsday. When Lilith found out there was a male demon baby who had been touched by Leila and Quelamia and one of the twins, the male, Lucifer's son, was still alive, she did not know which one had been touched and given the power. Her plans were destroyed.

"Therefore, Lilith immediately ordered the death of demons to destroy them all. But Lilith did not consider that the twins would have the power to control hell. They can open and lock most of the doors to hell. They are also unbelievable."

"There are six hundred sixty-six left," I heard Gabriellele murmur.

"What was that, Gabriellele?"

"I am one of them," she said in a much clearer voice.

"That is why you were telling me to stop Lilith," I said, finally understanding. I turned to Greg. "How can we stop them from getting hurt by Lilith and her demons? As you have said, they are all over the world."

"We would have to find the twins. The hard part is finding them because Leila destroyed all the files on these male babies at that hospital. Maybe Gabriellele can help you to find these people. As soon as we find them, we have to do a ceremony to drive out the evil spirits. This must be done on them dead or alive."

"As far as I know, there are different religions involved. Greg, do you know how to do it?"

"No, Viktoria," he said with a shake of his head. "They must have done what their religion required them to do. Jewish folklore and kabbalah teachings tell of a malevolent spirit called a dybbuk. This spirit is the soul of a dead person that has come back. It inhabits the body of a living person in order to carry out its goals. The dybbuk can be expelled through a rite of exorcism and leaves the body through the toes.

"Islamic belief tells of a jinn—an evil spirit and servant of Lucifer. They can invade the human body and cause illness, pain, and torment. Evil thoughts possess a person. One can make them expel the jinn by reciting particular passages of the Koran.

"In Hinduism, the Vedas scriptures tell of an evil spirit that can not only harm humans but can also stand in the way of the will of the gods. A traditional Hindu exorcism includes such rituals as burning pig excrement, reciting prayers, and offering sweets to the gods."

"Greg, what about the draining of blood like what happened to Gabriellele? She didn't have a single drop of blood remaining in her body. Forensics was shocked; there was not a toothmark or any kind of cut. How did that happen?"

"That was done by Lilith, I believe. She has been known to be a blood demon, and we know that vampires are blood demons as well. They can draw the blood out with their energy through the smallest break in the skin. You would need a microscope to actually see it."

"I cannot believe what I'm hearing! *Vampires*? That would be impossible!"

"Viktoria, as far as I remember, your father, Illia, wasn't he a jinn psychic? He used to talk to them and ask how to find out things. He can make them obey him. You could ask him for help. Ask him to send some of his good jinn, and we could have them obey you and help us fight on our side."

"Yes," I said, considering it. "I can ask my dad to help me; he always said that I could ask him for his good jinn at anytime. They will help me. I think now is the time to get some help. We'll instruct Babushka's jinns to obey us and asked them if they can amalgamate in the force with us."

"We can also do out-of-body traveling," Gabriellele added. "We might be able to find the twins as well. I have the power to tell the difference between the ranks of angels. I also sense that they will leave and try telepathy. It may work."

"Gabriellele's right, Viktoria; you can do that."

I got my purse and put the strap on my shoulder. "Thanks for everything. You have been a great help. About the good jinn, I'll leave it to my mom and dad. Even though they're not here physically, they're here spiritually. I know they still have those good ones around."

"That's excellent; we'll try to get help from the others as well."

"What do you mean by 'the others'? Who are they?"

"I meant the elders who can control the unknown and the angels as well demons, like Illia, your father."

"I should leave now. Brandon might get suspicious." We said our good-byes, and I walked to the car. Once I got in and started the car, I asked, "Gabriellele, why didn't you tell me about these things when I askcd you? Why did you hesitate?"

"Viktoria, I did not know that much, but when Greg explained it, it made sense. Yes, I was bitten by something where I had a small birthmark. There were teethmarks, less than half an inch between them. I felt it when the demon of death appeared as someone I hadn't seen for a long time. I meant to meet this person; he called me up and said he wanted to talk to me and asked if I could meet him at the corner to hang out together."

"Then what happened?"

"It was a setup." She shrugged. "You know the rest of the story."

I heard my phone ring and pulled it out. "It's Brandon. He must be worried that it has taken me so long." I answered the phone. "Hello?"

"Viktoria!" Brandon yelled. "Where are you? We are worried sick about you! We've tried calling you again and again! Why didn't you answer your phone at least?"

"I am so sorry, Brandon. I just remembered that my phone was off, and when I turned it on, you called me. I had to go to another pharmacy to get my medicine because the one I usually go to did not have it. Honey, I will see you soon; I am about two blocks away."

"Viktoria, please return. Michael has been calling you. He needs to talk to you."

"I will call him when I get home. Brandon, someone is on the other line. I bet it's Michael. I'll see you later."

"See you later."

# Chapter 3

## *Prayers*

"Hi, Michael," I said when I hung up with Brandon. "What's so urgent?"

"Friend of mine called and said there is a case we might be interested in. I told him our hands were full with the case we have now. Then he said there are two victims, both females. They died a week apart from each other. The thing is, their autopsy results are the same."

"I'm so glad you called. I've been having flashes of a huge white house. Do you know anyone whose name starts with W?"

"No, but this case is in Washington DC. Do you think you can stop by the station? Tomorrow?"

"Sure."

"Then see you early in the morning."

"Michael, can you please ask your friend if he can e-mail the pictures of the victims and their autopsy results? I will try to work on it tonight."

"All right, Viktoria, I will. It may take a little time for you to receive it."

"That's fine. I'll be home late anyway. I'm going out to celebrate my homecoming. I have to go now, but I will call back when I get the e-mail."

"Enjoy your outing."

"Why don't you join us, Michael?"

"Next time. I'm exhausted, but thanks for the offer."

"Okay then, we'll talk later. Bye for now."

"See you later, Viktoria."

When I finally got home, Cameron greeted me with, "Mommy is home!"

"I hope everyone is hungry and ready to go out, because I'm starving!"

"Where are we going?" Melisa asked.

"Anywhere that we don't have to wait long to eat," Lacey mumbled.

"You pick the restaurant," Brandon told me.

"Mom, can I have ice cream for dessert?" Cameron asked me.

"Only if you finish your food."

"How about if I eat half of it and take the rest home?"

"It's a deal, but only if you take half of your dessert home too."

"That's not fair!"

"Come on, Cameron," Melisa said as she grabbed her purse. "If we don't hurry up, we're not going to eat anything!"

"Let's move it, Brandon!"

"Did everyone decide? Where are we going?"

"Yes, Dad, we're going to Mommy's favorite Italian restaurant. They have the best cheesecake."

"Oh, Lacey, you know your mother best," I said with a smile, since that was where I had picked to eat.

*    *    *

While we ate, I felt someone watching us.

*There they are.*

It was hard to see, since we were right in the corner. I didn't think they knew I could see them.

Lacey replied, "Who are those two, Mom? Do you know them?"

"No, Lacey, I do not."

"Why are they staring at our table, Mom? No one else can see them! Look, the waiter just walked right through them!"

"I know, baby," I said in a whisper as I patted her hand. I then leaned over, so my mouth was near her ear. I made it look like I was kissing her temple. "We need to finish our dinner and get the hell out of here, before your father realizes you can see them too."

It was such a great night, apart from being watched. I felt their presence with us all the way back home as well.

As soon as we walked through the door, Brandon turned to me. "Viktoria, I'm going to bed. I need to get up early. I have a meeting."

"Okay, baby," I said as I gave him a kiss on the cheek. "I'm going to stay up a bit more. I need to go over some files and prepare some reports, and I need to get the kids ready for bed."

As soon as the others had all gone up to their rooms, Babushka appeared. "I am surprised to see you, Babushka," I said, concerned. "What are you doing here?"

"Viktoria, I'm here to tell you that those people you saw at the restaurant are here with you for your family's protection."

"Thank you, Babushka, but why would I need protection? Do you know something?"

"Well, since you are dealing with Lilith and jinn, I believe that you need protection. When Greg comes, these two jinn will obey you. I have to go now, but I will be back with more details."

"Okay, Babushka, I suppose you know what you're doing. Thanks for the warning." Once he was gone, I sighed. "Gabriellele, we need to talk," I said, walking into the kitchen to make a cup of cofee. "I know you have seen them. Do you know these two?"

"No, Viktoria, I did not know who they were until I heard your father tell you."

"You need to tell me more about yourself. When I went to meet your mother, you knew that was a setup, but how did you know?"

"I never liked that house. It always felt like hell; it never had light coming through. It always seemed inhuman, and I heard things. My parents never believed it. I had been told that I must be on drugs since

I was having delusions and nightmares. Even when they saw cuts and bruises, they just admitted me to mental institutions."

"Why did they hurt you?"

"No, not from my parents, demons! They did so many things to me. I could not go to the priest. I could not get help from them or any other man of religion.

"Every night, I attempted to get help; I knew they would hurt me more. Because I did not want anything else to happen, I memorized spells and did not tell anyone about it. They gave me instructions to manipulate all the men of religion and regular people as well. They wanted me to play with their minds or kill them! They wanted me to drink human blood. They carried on, saying, 'You are one of us! You have to obey us!' I knew I could not be like them; even though my parents never went to church, I had my beliefs, and good was on my side. I believed in God. I was not supposed to hurt anyone. Mom always told me 'Keep your journey in life good and clean,' and I know why they said that."

"Did you know you were adopted?"

"The first time I heard about it is when Mom told you."

"Gabriellele, I'm so sorry. What you have gone through! I promise to help you to see the good and go through that beautiful light." I started to yawn; I couldn't deny my body any longer. "I better hit the sack. Tomorrow is going to be a long day. Good night."

"Sleep well, Viktoria. I'll be watching over you and your family."

"Thanks, Gabriellele. I'm happy to know we are being watched by an angel like you."

*   *   *

It was six o'clock the next morning when I awoke. The sun had just come out. I could feel, before I even opened my eyes, that it was going to be a long day. All night, I'd had nightmares. There was one long-haired lady in particular in my dreams. She was beautiful; I think that it might possibly have been Lilith. My body was aching like someone had run me over with a truck.

When I turned to my right, I noticed that Brandon was already gone. I called out his name, but there was no response, so I got up to go downstairs. When I got to the bottom of the stairs, I saw Gabriellele standing there with an expression on her face that could only be described as horror. "What happened, Gabriellele?"

"Viktoria, when Brandon came out of the room, he looked straight at me as if he could see me! And his eyes were red!"

"That's impossible," I said with a shake of my head. "Maybe his eyes were wandering, and it felt like he could see you."

"You're right," she said, but she didn't sound sure. "It might have been like that."

"Is he in the kitchen now?"

"Brandon left an hour ago. He's going to get coffee."

"Then I will wake the rest of the gang," I said before going back upstairs to wake my children. I knocked on each of their doors and hollered, "Come on, kids! Get up! Breakfast should be ready in ten minutes!"

I went downstairs to start making breakfast. I was done making three French toasts by the time they started showing up one by one.

"Mom," Melisa asked as she took a bite of her food, "can I borrow your car today? My tires need to be rotated."

"I'll drop you off at school; I need my car today," I said as I put a plate of food in front of Lacey and Cameron.

"Okay, but we have to leave early. I have a class at ten after seven."

Once all my kids were ready to go, we got in the car. I dropped everyone off as I made my way to work. When I was almost there, I heard Gabriellele mumbling.

"Talking to me, Gabriellele?"

"I'm sort of talking about you but not to you."

"What do you mean?"

"You know the case Michael told you about? I suppose you're going to see Michael about it. Well, one of the victims in the case is here with us but not showing herself because she is scared."

"Oh, God, Gabriellele, how long has she been with us? How did she get here? How did that happen?"

"Last night after you went to bed, I started searching for her and I found her. I told her who you are and that you are the only one who can help us. She's been among us since this morning. Her name is Carmella."

"Why didn't I see her earlier?"

"Because she did not want to be seen. She wasn't ready. She just tagged along with us today so she can see if she is able to trust us."

"It's nice to meet you, Carmella. I'm sure together we will do what needs to be done. We're going over to the station now."

I pulled my car into the parking lot and then into a spot. "Okay, we're here. Remember to be aware of everything around you, and if you feel uncomfortable, let me know. You can also stay next to me if you both need me. Please just say my name, and I will help you."

We got out of the car and walked to the door. Once inside, I saw Michael. "Good morning, Michael. Did you get the reports from Washington?"

"Yes, they're right here. I have been going over the autopsy files. It's the same thing; her heart failed, and there was no blood left. She was driving when the heart attack occurred. But this happened weeks ago." He put the paper down and looked at me. "Viktoria, we need to go over there, because this case is exactly like the other one—the blood was drained out of the body."

"You mean, just like Gabriellele?"

"Autopsy shows that there was not a single drop of blood left in the body, and there is no sign of any cut."

"Then we don't have any time to waste. Let's go now to see the body. I believe we are dealing with more than one kind of demon."

"Viktoria, what are you saying? Who are they? What do they want from these people?"

"I'll tell you everything on the way there. Come on, let's go!"

"I can't believe my ears! I've never heard of any thing like this before. But how are we going to find these people?"

"You have to get files on all the deaths and disappearances," I said, changing the topic, since I didn't know quite how to answer him.

"What about the remaining six hundred sixty-four people? How are you going to find them if they're all over the world?"

"My friend Greg Cheveyo is a Native American demonologist who will come with us. We have to find them and protect them from Lilith, the jinn, and Lucifer."

"You mean we are dealing with demons?" he asked, shocked. "We don't know how to handle a situation like that!"

"You could say our hands are full with the demons. Luckily, we do know how to fight back and have people to back us up. When we get there, Michael, be sure to take pictures of anything suspicious. Look around the body to see if there is any kind of mark."

"I'll try to record anything out of the ordinary."

"Don't be scared of anything that happens or that might pop up. Make sure to have your cross showing and have this holy water handy. You'll also have to repeat a verse."

"Which is?"

"Repeat after me: 'There shall no demon touch me or hurt me. I am the creation of God, and I obey him; He is the father of Jesus. I shall be protected by him and the archangels sent by him.'"

"Why would we need all this for protection if they're both already dead?"

"We may need a ritual in case their bodies have been taken over by another demon. Then we need to do an exorcism and baptize them. Otherwise, the priest won't be able to bury them."

"Why do we baptize them?"

"Their mothers were impregnated by jinn. They are also servants of Lucifer. A priest, imam, or rabbi would not able to bury them. They will know that this is Lilith's doing. They cannot take a chance of a fight with Lilith or any jinn. Therefore, they will baptize them at the burial, or at the morgue."

"I'm going to get the jitters all ready," he said, walking away.

"Don't worry," I said, following him. "Greg's meeting us over there. We have the best demonologist on our side."

We decided to go in my car. Michael gave me directions as we drove. "We're here," he said when I pulled up to the morgue. "We need to see Captain Murray first; he's going to help us with this case and take us to the morgue."

"I see Greg is here too," I said as I got out of the car. "Let me get him caught up on the case." I walked over to him and greeted him with a smile. "I'm so glad you made it. We were going downstairs." I turned and saw Michael looking at me. I motioned for him to come closer. "Michael, I would like to introduce you to my friend Greg. Greg, this is Michael. Greg will join us if it's okay with Captain Murray."

"Why not?" Michael asked. "He can join us, Viktoria."

As we were going downstairs, Greg suddenly stopped.

"Why did you stop, Greg?"

"We have company, Viktoria."

"Who is it?"

"I believe it's Lilith. As to why she is here, we will soon find out."

Captain Murray opened the door. Before I could comprehend what Greg had just said, there was Lilith. She looked so evil, yet so beautiful. Now I understood how easy it was for her to seduce men.

As she passed by me, she whispered in my ear, "I am not finished yet. You cannot stop me. Even your God can't." Then she vanished.

Michael asked, "Who is she?"

Captain Murray replied, "Must be related to the deceased, but she is gorgeous!"

Greg and I approached the bodies. It was so strange; one person had died one week before the other one. Only it looked like nothing had happened to them; they still had their color. Suddenly, Greg pushed me away. He started spraying holy water and placed the crosses on them.

"Viktoria, these bodies have been possessed by demons! They knew we were coming. She's trying to stop us. Get the rest out of here or stay back; we need to do an exorcism."

Captain Murray rejected the idea. "They're dead!" he said.

"I'm a demonologist," Greg said. "Viktoria and I believe these two were killed by demons, and their bodies have been taken over by demons. If you come a bit closer, you will see they're still alive. This means that the body has been taken over by a demon or a lost soul."

Greg and Captain Murray approached the body. The captain moved his hand closer. Her eyes were wide open, and when he got close enough to her, she pulled him toward her and said, "Try to get rid of me."

"Oh Lord, this is not real! You must be kidding me!" the captain yelled, becoming terrified. "Is she still alive? What the hell is that? She even spoke to me. Did you hear what she said?"

"Yes, we did," I said. "No, we're not joking; if you read the autopsy, you would have seen that she has been dead for a couple of days now. The blood has been drained from the bodies, but there were no scars or cuts."

"Let me see those records," he demanded. When Greg handed them over, Captain Murray looked at them for a long time. Finally, he said, "You're right. Do you think this was caused by a vampire?"

"Wouldn't there have been fang marks on the body? But there was no sign of any. Only the queen of bloodsuckers, the demon Lilith, would be able to do this. This is how we're going to find out: check the mouth for any loose teeth. This is how they draw out the blood of their victims. She is the head demon of vampires. Lillin, her daughter, is one of the commanders of the vampires."

"You know, Greg, if I had not seen this with my own eyes, I would not believe you. But go ahead; do whatever you need to do."

Greg and I started the exorcism first, since the body had been taken over. As soon as Greg put the cross on the victim's forehead, she hissed and jumped at us. We continued to spray holy water and commanded the demon to leave the body. It would not respond to our command.

"Michael, what are the victims' names and religions?" I asked.

"Check her toe," he told us. "She should have a tag."

We moved down to her feet, pulled back the sheet that was covering her, and looked at her foot. "Greg, her name is Azalea; she is Jewish. We have to do it their way."

Captain Murray replied, "I know someone, Rabbi Rubenstein. Let me call him; he lives close by. He might be able to help us."

While the captain made the phone call, Greg tried to explain how the Jewish exorcism ritual had to be performed by a rabbi who had mastered practical kabbalah.

"The ceremony involves a quorum of ten people."

"Ten people?" Captain Murray said. "We can't do this over here."

Greg replied, "We have to do it here; we cannot move her. It's too dangerous. There is too much risk. We need those ten to gather in a circle around the possessed person. The group recites a psalm three times, and the rabbi blows the shofar—a ram's horn. They blow the ram's horn in a certain way, with certain notes, in an effort to shatter the body, so to speak, so that the soul that is possessed can be shaken loose. After it has been shaken loose, they can begin to communicate with the demon and ask it what its purpose for being here is."

"Do you really think it will communicate?" the captain asked doubtfully.

"Well," said Greg, "don't be so pessimistic. If it doesn't, they can pray and do a ceremony for the soul to feel safe. Then they will baptize her. We need Rabbi Rubenstein over here as soon as possible."

After a minute of silence, Michael asked me, "Viktoria, you're not serious, are you? There is no way they will let us do this. We need permission from the family and the DA. No one can perform exorcisms in a morgue."

"What about it, Captain Murray? You have given us permission. We don't have time, Greg, to find her family, but you could get whatever you need before the rabbi comes or let us do what we need to do."

While we were waiting for Rabbi Rubenstein, Father Johnson joined us, and we started the other victim's exorcism.

"In the name of Jesus Christ, our Lord and God, by the intercession of Mary, spotless Virgin and Mother of Jesus, of St. Michael the Archangel, of the blessed apostles Peter and Paul, and of all the saints, and by the authority residing in our holy ministry, we steadfastly proceed to combat the onslaught of the wily enemy." Father Johnson's voice started to tremble audibly, though he tried to hide it, and bullets of sweat dripped down his forehead, but he continued with a trembling voice: "God arises; His enemies are scattered, and those who hate him flee before him. As smoke is driven away, so are they driven; as wax melts before the fire, so the wicked perish before God."

As he finished his speech, Father Johnson was blown backward. He asked Greg if he could help him with the rest of verse. They said, "See the cross of the Lord; be gone, you hostile powers! The stem of David, the lion of Judah's tribe has conquered. May your mercy, Lord, remain with us always. For we put our whole trust in you. We cast you out, every unclean spirit, every Lucifer in power, every onslaught of the infernal adversary. Every legion, every diabolical group and sect, in the name and by the power of our Lord Jesus Christ, we command you, be gone and fly far from the Church of God, from the souls made by God in—"

I felt Lilith's presence and knew things were getting worse. Father Johnson had to stop for a moment.

I asked him if we could get someone who had the same knowledge to come assist them.

Father Johnson shook his head as he said, "No," and continued with, "His image and redeemed by the precious blood of the divine Lamb. I can see, Father. No longer dare, conger serpent, to deceive the human race, to persecute God's Church, to strike God's elect, and to sift them as wheat. For the Most High God commands you, He to whom you once proudly presumed yourself equal; He who wills all men to be saved and come to the knowledge of truth. God, the Father, commands you. The Son of God commands you. God, the Holy Ghost, commands you. Christ, the eternal Word of God made flesh, commands you, who humbled himself, becoming obedient even unto death, to save our race from the perdition wrought by your envy; who founded His Church upon a firm rock, declaring that the gates of hell should never prevail against her, and that He would remain with her all days, even to the end of the world. The sacred mystery of the cross commands you, along with the power of all the mysteries of the Christian faith. The exalted Virgin Mary, Mother of Jesus, commands you, who in her lowliness crushes your proud head from the first moment of her Immaculate Conception. The faith of the holy apostles Peter and Paul and the other apostles commands you. The blood of martyrs and the devout prayers of all holy men and women command you.

"Therefore, accursed dragon and every diabolical legion, we adjure you by the living God, by the true God, by the holy God, by God, who so loved the world that He gave His only begotten Son, that whoever believes in him might not perish but—"

Things where not looking good, and I was starting to worry. It was getting ugly as Father Johnson continued, "… have everlasting life; to cease deluding human creatures and filling them with the poison of everlasting damnation; to desist from harming the Church and hampering her freedom. Be gone, Lucifer, father and master of lies, enemy of man's welfare. Give place to Christ, in whom you found none of your works. Give way to the one, holy, catholic, and apostolic Church, which Christ himself purchased with His blood. Bow down before God's mighty hand, tremble and flee as we call on the holy and awesome name of Jesus, before whom the denizens of hell cower, to whom the heavenly Virtues and Powers and Dominations are subject, whom the Cherubim and Seraphim praise with unending cries as they sing: 'Holy, holy, holy, Lord God of Sabbath.'

"Lord, heed my prayer. And let my cry be heard by you. The Lord is with me. May He also be with you. Let us pray."

We all started to pray. "God of heaven and earth, God of the angels and archangels, God of the patriarchs and prophets, God of the apostles and martyrs, God of the confessors and virgins, God who has power to bestow life after death and rest after toil; for there is no other God than you, nor can there be another true God beside you, the Creator of all things visible and invisible, whose kingdom is without the end; we humbly entreat your glorious majesty to deliver us by your might from every influence of the accursed spirits, from their every evil snare and deception, and to keep us from all harm; through Christ our Lord. Amen."

As Greg and Father Johnson were spraying the holy water, the demon was reacting. "You will never get rid of us until we are done with the rest of them!"

"From the snares of the devil, Lord, deliver us," Father Johnson continued. "That you help your church to serve you in security and freedom. We beg you to hear us. That you humble the enemies of the holy church. We beg you to hear us!"

Suddenly, black smoke began to roll out of her mouth. It vanished as suddenly as it had appeared. The demon finally left Carmella's body. Then the priest baptized her, and as soon as we were done, the victim looked so calm and so peaceful.

When we finished with Carmella, Captain Murray came up to us. "What are these marks on the victims? Only holy water burns?"

"Don't worry, Captain Murray," I said. "A few little burns from the holy water. This happens when the body is obtained by evil spirits. With makeup, the families will never notice them."

"When are the victims' families coming to see them, Captain Murray?" Greg asked.

"The family of one of the victims will be here this afternoon, but we could not find the other's family. When she was found, there was no identification except her hospital internship ID. We got the address from the personnel office, but, unfortunately, the address they gave us was not the right one. We're still searching for her next of kin."

"Would you have a copy of the address?"

"Yes." He went to get the address out of a file and talked as he searched, "It's strange. Maybe it was some sort of mistake made by the hospital. There must be another address."

"Michael, why don't you call the hospital? They might be able to find the proper address."

"Sure, Viktoria," he said as he pulled out his cell phone. "I'll call them up now."

"Michael," I said, "ask them if she had a friend or anyone else close to her. They might know where she lived."

Suddenly, the door opened, and a black could of smoke entered the room. The captain panicked and started to yell, "Fire!"

Greg yelled to him, "It's not a fire! It's a demon's spirit trying to stop the rabbi from entering the room!"

The captain looked so frightened; he was shaking and kept mumbling, "What the hell are we dealing with?"

When the rabbi walked in with his crew, they saw the black smoke all over the room. By the look of Rabbi Rubenstein and the others, I was sure they had seen their share of such occurrences. This was nothing new to them.

Rabbi Rubenstein hesitated to go ahead with the exorcism at first. They did not want to deal with Lilith until the captain nicely told them they had no choice.

The rabbi and his crew put the victim on top of the table. He asked us to leave and watch the exorcism through the window for our safety.

We went outside. Once we were safely on the other side, they started it. It was extremely interesting. It was the first time Greg and I had seen a different tradition's exorcism.

I looked at Captain Murray's face; he looked fascinated and also scared.

The exorcism took about five hours, and some parts of it were terrifying. Once it was almost over, the rabbi told us to come in and ask the demon the question we needed to ask it. We all went in; Greg and I moved closer to the victim. Greg asked the question. The demon soul said repeatedly, "I serve Lilith and the jinn. I am a servant of Lucifer." Then the demon left the body.

Afterward, the rabbi continued with the baptism.

When I went outside, I heard Azalea ask, "Why can't I go to the light now? Why are they stopping me?"

"Azalea, you will be escorted to the light by Leila, as soon as we find the remaining six hundred sixty-four. We will need to know everything to help us fight Lilith and the demon to save the rest of them."

"Viktoria," Michael said as he came outside, "I just finished talking to hospital personnel. They gave me the same address. Why do they have this one in their system?"

"Greg and I are going over there now. If anyone wants to join us, they are welcome."

"After what I have seen today, nothing will keep me away." He started walking to his car before asking me, "Viktoria, do you need a marked car to come with you?"

"That's not necessary at this point. Thanks anyway."

Captain Murray then came out, putting on his jacket. "Wouldn't miss this for the world! I'm coming with you, Michael."

"Sure, why not?"

"Viktoria, you go with Greg," Michael said, getting into his car. "I'll follow you."

"Okay then, let's go!"

As I walked to the car, I felt someone with us. I noticed Gabriellele, but the rest were no longer with us.

"Greg, do you feel what I feel?"

"Yes. Get the holy water and the cross out."

As I reached into my bag, which I had placed on the backseat of the car, I saw my mom. "What are you doing here?"

"Dad wanted to talk to you," she said, in reference to my father. "He said you might need some help."

"Where is Dad?" I asked as I started the engine.

"You'll see him when you get to the place. For now, I will guide you."

As Greg opened the door, I realized that I had disregarded my manners. "I don't know if you've met Greg," I said to Mom.

"We've met," she said.

"Viktoria, you have to be careful," she said as I started driving. "Lilith is very dangerous. She might harm you or the family. That's why we have been sent by Quelamia to find the rest of Lucifer's babies. Any missteps, and we will have an early doomsday."

"What are you saying?" I asked.

"What doomsday?"

"Honey, when I say doomsday, I mean the battle between angels and demons. When Lilith was rejected by God because she refused to obey Adam, she swore that she would kill all the angels, and God punished her by taking her demon children fathered by Lucifer. This is all about getting back at God, by opening all the doors to hell so she could free all the demons."

"I feel someone is here," Greg said.

"Yes, I do too. And it's not my dad."

"I know, but I just wanted to see where they would take us."

"Is Azalea ready for this?" I asked. He shrugged. "Okay, we're here."

"Viktoria, there is nothing here but dumps."

"Where are we, Michael?"

"We are at the address that was given to us."

"Greg, call Michael and tell him not to get out of the car. We need to turn back. This is a setup."

"Miss Viktoria, what's going on?" I heard someone ask.

"Greg, stop! Don't go any further! Look, there's black smoke! We can't drive right into that, or they will drag us into the hole! This is a setup!"

"Viktoria," my mom said, "do not get out of the car! That is not Dad!"

"Okay, don't worry; we won't go any closer."

"Remember the verse from the Koran. Pray and that verse will demolish the jinn."

"Yes, I do remember, and I see him." I started repeating a verse. "I seek refuge in Allah from you. I curse you by Allah's curse. I curse you by Allah's curse. I curse you by Allah's curse."

As soon as I finished with the verse, the jinn vanished with it.

"Gabriellele," I asked, "is Azalea with us?"

"Viktoria, how did you do it?" she asked, amazed. "They vanished! Did you know you'd been set up again? She's not your mother; she is a jinn!"

"I better call Lacey," I said pulling out my phone. "Since she also has this power I possess, she might have felt that something was wrong. She must be having a panic attack by now." When she picked up her phone, I asked, "Lacey, is everything okay over there? How is the rest of the family?"

"We're fine. Don't worry. Dad called. He had to go out of state; he has an emergency meeting. He said he'll be back tomorrow. Dad also said he called you and left a message on your cell."

"He never mentioned anything about a meeting," I said, racking my brain to see if I might have forgotten it. "Otherwise, I would never have left you kids alone."

"We'll be fine, Mom. Get back to work."

"Okay. I love you."

"I love you too," she said before we hung up. As soon as I disconnected, my phone rang again. "Captain Murray, I told you at the beginning that we are dealing with demons," I said when I heard him having a panic attack.

"There is nothing here but the dump! Look at that house; it's unlivable. Who would live there?"

"Yes, I know, Captain Murray, but you are the one who gave us this address."

"This address was on her employee records. Even Michael checked it, if I remember right."

I felt another presence among us. I knew instantly who it was. "Azalea, this is the address shown on your work files."

"I don't know who changed the address," she said, confused. "But I live seven miles away from here."

I turned to Greg. "I just had a communication from Azalea. She said she lives seven miles away from here." I spoke into my phone. "Can I talk to Michael?"

"Yes, hold on."

"What is going on, Viktoria?" Michael asked.

"Michael, we can't trust the address that was given to us. It was a setup by Lilith to stop us! I believe she is doing a good job at it too. One of the victims, Azalea, was telling me that she lived seven miles away from here."

"Are we going there?"

"I can't take a chance; it's too risky. We need to go back to New York. My kids are alone; Brandon has gone out of state."

"We'll meet at the airport then."

"Michael, our flight is at 9:30 at night; I cannot wait that long. I'll be returning with Greg. If you would like to, you can come with us."

"Okay, I'll come with you. We'll meet at the station."

"Wait there for me, Michael."

"Greg," I said, hanging up the phone, "that was not my mom, and that is not my dad. She never called me, 'honey'; she always called me 'baby.' Also, she never met you before, but she said she did. I always called my dad, 'Babushka,' and she never mentioned that. She used the word *dad*." As I finished babbling, I asked, "Greg, did you ever meet my parents?"

"I met your father once, but I never met your mom."

"Look at the surroundings," I said, referring to the disaster pit we were staring at. "It's a dump. This is where jinns mostly live."

"Thank God, Viktoria, that you figured it out in time. I don't want to think about what could have happened!"

"I can't believe they used my mom and dad! We have to be more careful. They could use my kids as well! They need better protection."

"You're right. Even I could not tell that was a jinn. I didn't know that they could impersonate another person so well. By the way, how did you get rid of them?"

"I remembered a verse from the Koran. As soon as I repeated the verse, the jinn vanished."

"Wow. You have to teach me that; I might need it one day. It seemed very powerful."

"Let's move on; it's getting late. We need to go back and pick up Michael from the station. It will be better if the kids aren't home alone; plus, I need to do the astral one-way. We need to find these people fast."

When we got back to the station, Greg unbuckled his seat belt. "I'm going upstairs to get Michael while you wait here."

"Okay, but tell him to hurry up."

About five minutes later, Greg came back with Michael. "You see? That was not long now, was it?"

I shook my head. "Let's go back home."

"Azalea," I said to the spirit in the back seat, "you can take me to the place where you lived. With astral travel, I might get more answers this way. Maybe we will see your parents."

"Viktoria, my parents live in Tel Aviv."

"I know. This astral travel can be done in spirit, but we need your help."

"I lived by myself here and do not have any other family members. I was going to visit home this summer … until Samuel took over my body."

"Azalea, you can see your parents now."

"Yes," Greg said. "Don't be scared; they cannot see you, unless you want them to touch you."

"Can I feel my mom?"

"Of course," I said with a nod. "You can see her as well, right, Greg?"

"Azalea, do you know why this happened to you? Were you aware of things like Gabriellele?"

"Yes, I do. My adopted parents always told me I was different, and they never took me to the temple with them. When I asked why, they said the rabbi would not allow them to enter the temple with me because I was the creation of shedim."

"Did you know what shedim meant?" I asked.

"I never knew what it meant until I was thirteen. My biological mother made them swear they would not tell me the truth until I turned thirteen. My adopted mother told me that it was not my mother's fault. She was an angel. It was all my grandparents' fault.

"My mother's parents were so sinful. They sacrificed their virgin daughter to shedim for their sins. A few months later, she found out that she was expecting a baby. Then she remembered when she was given to shedim; she had fallen into a deep sleep the night that she was a raped by a demon. She felt the shame, she said.

"She had tried to have an abortion but could not do it, so she decided to put me up for adoption. Right after that, she threw herself down from a cliff. The police never found her body. My adopted parents kept this a secret for a while. My adopted mom begged the rabbi to do an exorcism, but he could not do it. He said he even attempted to do it by himself, but that was impossible. He couldn't get people to help him either, because they were all aware of the consequences."

"Did you have any experiences like Gabriellele's? Did you see them face-to-face?"

"Yes, I did. They also taught me how to vanquish an angel or any demonologist or clairvoyant who came close to finding out about doomsday so they would die mysteriously, just the way it was done to us by Lilith. We also got people to change their religions. I would do anything to try to erase everything they told me to believe and everything they told me to disbelieve."

"What else did they do to you?"

"They taught us the most important thing: the verse for doomsday, which we had to memorize. We were told that one day, when we were ready, we were going use it. They made us do things that we did not want to do."

"What did they make you do?"

"I was forced to drink human blood. I tried to refuse to drink it, but they would hurt me or punish me. When I told my parents, they could not do anything about it. The only thing they could do was send me away after I finished high school. So I have been living here and never went back to my country."

"So you are also some kind of vampire like Lilith? Did you ever willingly kill anyone or bite anyone? Did these lessons continue over here too?"

"Yes, they did. I had no choice but to do what they told me to do, but most of the time, I was not willing. They told me I had no choice; my career in the medical field was excellent. I was highly ranked, because I had converted so many people to their side. Then I was to join in the Freemasons. Power was given to me. I had a job as I continued with my college. As long as I converted people to worship Lilith and Lucifer, I joined the rich and well-educated people in masonry.

"When I fell in love with Rabbi Leon, I told him everything. He said he might be able to help me whenever I decided to stop dealing with Lilith. I started studying Judaism. I did not want to continue anymore. They said they would take everything away from me, or they would hurt Rabbi Leon.

"The night of my death, the demon of death, disguised as Rabbi Leon, asked me to meet him at the side of the temple. I thought he called me to help me get out of this awful thing. When I went there to see him, he said he had good news and that I would be happy to hear it. He came closer and gave me a hug. I felt him going right through my body. Then he put his hand right through to my heart and clutched it. He said, 'We don't need you anymore,' and the demon took over my body. The rest you know."

# Chapter 4

## Carmella's Baby

"Azalea, did you see Carmella around?"

"No," Azalea answered. "I have not felt her presence yet."

"Viktoria," Gabriellele said, "Carmella went to see her baby."

"What?" I asked, completely thrown. "She has a baby?"

"Carmella had an affair with a married man. When she became pregnant, he told her to have an abortion. She refused, and he left. She thought he was infertile. He said that the baby could not be his. Since then, she has not seen him."

"Gabriellele, do you think we may perhaps be able to find her?"

"I don't know, but Azalea and I will try."

"Greg," I said, "the next stop is a rest area. We need to use the map and the crystal to find Carmella. Michael will drive." I looked at the time. "I need to call Brandon." I picked up my phone and was about to dial when it rang. "Speak of the devil." I picked up, "Hi, honey, I was just talking about you."

"Hope it was good," he joked.

"Always. By the way, where are you? Lacey said you were out of town?"

"Yes, honey, I called you, but you didn't pick up your phone, so I left a message. I'm in Virginia. Do you member the big project I've been working on? Well, we need to sign the contract as soon as possible, and I decided not wait. My mom should be with the kids. I asked her to go over there and stay until you come."

"If I knew you were going to Virginia, I would have met you at home. When Lacey called, she didn't mention your mom coming over."

"Shoot, I forgot to tell them about it. I hope they didn't panic."

"I don't think so. They'll be very happy to see her. Anyway, I should be home in a few hours."

"Where did you go?"

"Washington DC. There was a case I needed to handle there. I thought it would not take long, but it did."

"What was the case that was so important you had to leave in a rush?"

"Oh nothing," I lied. "A politician wanted a consultation. You know how they are; they want everything to a T. Honey, I have to go now; my cell phone battery is dying. We'll talk when you get home. Love you. Take care." And before he could say anything, I hung up.

"Viktoria, why did you lie to Brandon?" Michael asked. "Why didn't you tell him the truth?"

"You know, he has been complaining lately that I am dealing with demons and death too much. I just did not want to upset him. Please, Michael, don't say anything, okay?"

"All right, Viktoria. It's just he's worried and concerned about you and the family especially. After what happened last night, you can't blame the guy."

I could sense the presence of Gabriellele. She seemed very concerned.

"I think you're right, Greg. About Gabriellele—she does sound worried."

"Gabriellele, is that you? Why can't I see you? What is it? Are you okay?"

"Just listen. Azalea and I are still watching over Carmella. Something happened. We think Carmella took over her grandmother's body."

"Are you saying she killed her grandmother?" I almost screamed. "Why would she do that?"

"Because of her baby. Carmella did not want to leave the baby with anyone. She kept saying she was not ready to die and that her baby needed her."

"We can do a lot now; she should be okay as long as there are no demon activities and she and the baby are safe," Greg said.

"Michael," I asked, "do you have Carmella's grandmother's phone number in the file? I think I may have seen her number."

"Yes, we do have it; it's the house number."

"I need to call that number, but she might endanger the baby's life."

When I called her, she picked up the phone. She sounded like her grandmother.

"Carmella, this is Viktoria. I know what you did. You know you have put your baby in danger this way. They will find you! Let your grandmother go back into her body. Your baby will be safer with her; trust me, we will take care of them."

"I don't know, Viktoria. I can't leave my baby. She needs me. I have to protect her. I am the only one who can do that."

"Listen to me, Carmella, your soul in your grandmother's body will lose its powers. They know you are dead! There is no reason why they would come after you. However, if they realize what is going on, they will come after you and the baby, and they will hurt both of you. You will not have the power to fight back. Think about it; I have to go now, but please, you have to do this for your baby and her safety." I hung up and turned to Greg. "We have to go back and talk to Carmella; she's in danger. She needs to be warned and has to realize what she has done."

"Viktoria, what happens if she refuses?"

I shook my head, thinking about her other options. "There has to be another way for her to stay around her baby but without taking her grandmother's body. Greg, do you know any other way to keep her around her baby?"

"The only person who will know is your father, Viktoria. He might be able to help her out. Try calling him."

I felt his presence the second Greg said "father."

"Well, we don't have to. He is here among us. Hi, Babushka, we were just talking about you."

"I know. I was with you the whole time; I know what's going on. Viktoria, you have to tell Carmella to go to the hospital close to her house. There will be a body waiting for her."

"Who is it, Babushka?"

"Don't worry, Viktoria. It is a homeless old lady who passed away. Carmella can take over her place. Anyway, the person in question resembles her grandmother, and no one will be able to tell the difference; they may think it is her great aunt. Call her back. Tell her I will be there waiting for her. You don't have to go all the way to where her grandmother lives."

"Thanks, Babushka, you've been a great help. I'll call her and tell her." I called Michael again. "Michael, turn back; we are going home. Carmella will be just fine with my dad. She was adopted by her grandma; she is only fifty-five."

"What happened to her parents?" Michael asked.

"Her mother died from a drug overdose. That was when her grandmother decided to adopt her."

"What about Carmella's father? Where is he?"

"He died in a car accident before her mother found out she was pregnant. Carmella was in her last year in law school, doing an internship in a well-known law firm. That firm is owned by that cult.

"I know that firm. Brandon worked with them for a while as a consultant. There was a case in which a psychiatrist and the hospital were sued for three hundred million dollars. Brandon was one of the evaluators. They gave it to the defendant due to the plaintiff's mental condition.

"He was suing the psychiatrist for being evil and worshiping demons. He also said that he saw a sacrifice of humans. That was over twenty years ago."

"I remember that, Viktoria. I even went to the hospital where all that sacrificing was supposed to have happened, but we could not find anything. Both the law firm and the hospital were and still are owned by the cult."

"I wonder if Carmella's baby's father was a client from that firm."

"Someone is working with her," I muse to Michael.

"Michael, remind me to call Carmella tomorrow and find the files for that lawsuit. I'm going to try to see if I can find anything else on that."

"You know what, Viktoria?" Greg asked. "Not too long ago, I heard a rumor about that hospital; patients were dying there. They had some mysterious deaths there, but they never filled out the death certificates."

"When was that, Greg?"

"A long time ago. One of the patients' families complained about how their mother had seen unusual things. They asked me if I could go and see her and perhaps talk to her about what she had seen. They wanted to know if I could find out if she had been possessed by any sort of demon."

"Then what happened? Was she possessed?"

"I never did find out; she passed away the morning her family and I went to see her. However, if you ask for my opinion, her death was unusual. She had her arms stretched out like she was on the cross, as if she was trying to protect herself from some sort of demon. It was totally mysterious."

"You know, Viktoria," Michael said, "we should check that hospital over. Let's see what we can find out about it. It creeps me out already."

"You can say that again. That's a good idea; we'll look into it."

"I see Gabriellele approaching, guys," I said as I watched her coming near us. "Yes, Gabriellele?"

"We're going by your house. We'll meet you over there; I know you're worried about your kids."

"All right," I said, letting out a sigh of relief. My mind could rest now. "Thank you, Gabriellele. You know Lacey is sensitive and can see you; can you tell her I'm on my way? Also my mother-in-law will be there, so just be careful. She has a history of panicking. Try not to scare her."

"Don't worry. We'll just watch over them through the window."

"You know what, Greg? Gabriellele and Azalea are the best demon ghosts ever; they even have concern for the kids. I would never have imagined that."

I looked around. "They went over there now."

"Viktoria, what happens with Carmella?"

"Well, Greg, apparently, she had a newborn baby, and she was not ready to leave her with anyone, even her grandmother. Somehow, Carmella took over her grandmother's body and is now taking care of her baby with her new identity. I hope she will listen to us before Lilith and her demons find out."

"Oh, my God, Viktoria! Can spirits go into someone else's body? How common is that?"

"Michael, not all spirits will do it; only the ones who feel like they were not ready yet. Like Carmella. Unfortunately, even demons can take over."

"This can happen not only with a dead body; it can also happen when psychics do astral traveling. It's usually called an out-of-body experience."

"What is that?"

"It is spiritually traveling places when you are in a deep sleep—which I will be doing with this case; Greg can also join me. When we need to find out more information, you can join or watch us."

"Viktoria, I am not over the exorcism yet. I don't think my heart can take another spiritual phenomenon. What I am saying is thanks but no thanks. I have had my share of nightmares today. This was enough for the rest of my life."

"We're almost home. Who should I drop off first? Michael? Oh, Michael, before you go in, don't forget to hold your cross and spray yourself with holy water. It's just for your safety."

"What do you mean? Can they follow us?"

"I'm not saying they did. I just mean in case they did, just do what I am telling you to do."

"Viktoria, for my safety keep your phone next to your bed in case of emergency."

"What do you mean? What sort of emergency?"

"I mean MRFHL."

"What is that?"

"Michael running for his life."

"Haaahaaa, funny!"

"I am glad you found this amusing, Viktoria, but I am serious."

"Good night, Michael."

"You can drop me off first and come inside to do the thing with me. Then I really need to go home, get a rest, and get my reports ready for tomorrow."

"Michael, I might show up late to work tomorrow. I have to drop the kids off at school."

"That's fine. I'll probably show up late myself," Michael said as he got out of the car. "Be safe." He closed the door and walked to his house. Once I saw that he was safely inside, I drove on.

"Greg, something is stuck in my head. It's about the law firm and the hospital; do you think there were all these rituals because of the cult? WL and L?"

"I don't know, Viktoria. I heard a lot of things about that organization, but there was not one bit of proof that they might be involved. It is a well-known and respected organization; all the members are highly educated people. I suppose they would not do anything to put the organization in the spotlight like that. Why do you ask?"

I sighed. "I don't know, but I know someone who may able to answer our questions."

"Who?"

"Brandon. We'll ask him who the WL and L are, what they do, and what their ritual is."

"If he does know, do you think he will tell us? These kinds of people swear on their life not to say a word."

"Maybe you're right, but it still would not hurt to ask. If he does not want to talk about it, I'll know he is probably involved."

"Why would you say that now, Viktoria?"

"Greg, how long you have known me?"

"About thirty-two years."

"You know that when I married Brandon, we had nothing. But when he started working for that law firm, we got a house, a brand-new car, and a boat. All these things in one year; I want to know how he did it."

"Viktoria, I think you are over-questioning yourself. Brandon was lucky with that law firm; he did well, and they paid him for his services. There is nothing wrong with that. Brandon is a hardworking and well-respected person; you're judging him too harshly."

"When we get to my place, come inside to make sure that there is no unwanted presence. And we can do the sage; I think we all need to relax."

"I need to ask you a question. I know you said you don't want to worry Brandon, that he did not want you to get involved in a case like this. Is there anything else you don't want to share?"

"Honestly, there is something that has been bothering me a lot, but I don't know why."

"What is it?"

"Since this case started, he has been rejecting my work and sort of telling me I should back down and not get involved. He tells me that it's dangerous and it might harm the kids."

"Maybe he's right to worry about you. And you should protect the kids first; I can't argue with that."

"I don't think he has ever complained about my work before. What does he know? Also why were Lilith's soldiers guarding him? I cannot stop wondering about that; it bothers me."

"What do you mean, Lilith's soldiers?"

"I mean jinns. When I was in the hospital that night, I had a premonition that there was a bad entity, and I decided to go home. I did it spiritually. When I entered the house, all my religious symbols were upside down, and the jinns were in front of my bedroom door guarding it. I don't know what to think of it." I pulled into my driveway. "We're home. Greg, you're still coming in, right?"

"Viktoria, look straight at the basement window."

"What is that? Brandon's shadow?"

"I thought I saw a black shadow; it looked like Brandon coming out of your basement."

"That's impossible. Brandon is staying in Virginia and will not be back until late afternoon. Get the holy water, the Bible, and the cross."

"Viktoria, do you have your small Koran? We might need it for jinns."

"Right here in my bag. Greg, let's do it quietly. I don't want to scare the kids or my mother-in-law. If she hears even a little noise, she will have all of the NYPD over in our backyard."

"Viktoria, start chanting for Gabriellele; she might be able to help us. Better if she goes down and checks around in the basement to make sure everything is okay."

I walked as close to the basement door as I dared. "Gabriellele, is that you in the basement?" I listened hard. "Greg, I'm not getting any responses from her. She's not here."

"Viktoria, chant again. I can feel something around here; we might need help."

"Viktoria," I heard a woman say, "it's us, Gabriellele and Azalea. Do not be afraid. We heard noises outside and were just checking."

It always intrigued me how Gabriellele was more serious and Azalea seemed to be more of the worrying type.

"Thank God, it's you! I was worried! There was a shadow in the basement, and Greg and I came out to investigate. But it must have been you girls."

"We didn't come out of the basement; we came from the front. Those lights were not on before."

"Okay, everyone," I said, "let's go inside and try not to scare anyone. Greg, you come, but you two," I looked at Gabriellele and Azalea, "keep away from there. It's too risky. Let's go."

Greg followed me to the front of the house. "I still say that was Brandon's shadow."

"I told you it could not be Brandon! It's impossible since he is not here."

"I thought I saw him earlier, about an hour go," Azalea said.

"What? When did you see him?"

"I went upstairs to talk to Lacey, and he was coming out of your room. She called him, but he was in a rush and did not stop."

"Let's go inside. There has to be some kind of explanation. I will ask Lacey if anything unusual happened; she is sensitive and might feel it." Just before we entered the house, I pulled out my phone. "I will call Brandon and see what he has to say." I dialed his number and waited for him to pick up. When he did, I said, "Hi, honey, just called to say I got home. How was your day? How did it go with the contract?"

"Just fine," he said. His voice sounded the same, nothing unusual. "We did sign the contract. I'm about to hit the sack, so hug the kids for me and tell them I miss them. I love you all, and I'll see you tomorrow."

"Okay, honey. I'm exhausted as well. I need to go to bed early too. The kids love you, and we will see you tomorrow." I hung up and turned to the group. "Brandon is still over there and sounded tired. So, what we saw could not have been him."

"Okay, Viktoria, you know what you should do? Get everyone out of the house. Let's throw some holy water around the basement because we saw the something down there."

I nodded and went to the door. Once I unlocked it, I opened it up and yelled, "Hi, kids! Mommy is home! How is everything going?"

"Look, Cameron, Greg came to see you!" Melisa said when she walked in.

"I see Grandma Nelly is here too," I noted when I saw her sitting in the living room.

"Mom, we're hungry!" Cameron said. "Can we go out to eat?"

"No, baby, I'm exhausted. But if it's okay with you guys, call the restaurant and order some food. Grandma Nelly will take you all and go pick up the food while I get changed."

"Mommy? Hey, Mommy?"

"Yes, Cameron, you don't need to repeat yourself; I know what you want."

"Okay then, tell me what I want," he said with a grin.

He thought I didn't know, but a mother knows everything about her children.

"Ice cream," I said with a smile.

"Wow, Mom! How did you know?"

"I think I want some ice cream too, so if you behave, Grandma Nelly might take you all to the ice cream place to buy your favorite ice cream as well."

"What do you think, Grandma Nelly? Would you be able to take them?"

"I think that is an excellent idea, Viktoria."

"I'll call the restaurant to place the order. It should be ready when you all get there. Also, kids, don't ask for anything else from Grandma Nelly, do you understand?"

"Yes, Mom," was the unanimous answer.

"What about ice cream?" Cameron asked.

"I'll handle that," Grandma Nelly answered with a smile.

"Thanks, Grandma."

Once everyone was ready, they left the house. I waved as I watched them. Then I turned around. "Greg, they've left. Let's start the siege. It will take them about an hour, so we have to be quick."

"Which way to the basement?"

"The basement is this way; follow me. Do we need to bring the holy water?"

"Yes, we do. I don't see Gabriellele or Azalea."

"I'm here," Azalea said. "But Gabriellele has gone somewhere."

"Did she say where she was going?"

"No, but she said she had some unfinished business to attend to."

"Okay. Azalea, we want you to stay around us."

"Actually, you are one of them. When they ask you, tell them you are here to stop us from trying to take them upstairs into the back room. We have everything ready. I'll be waiting."

"Okay, but, Greg, wouldn't they know that I am not one of them? On the other hand, what if they recognize me?"

"No, I don't think so. Use your powers to vanquish them. Make yourself just like them so they will not think you're different."

"Viktoria, I feel their presence."

"We're going to go downstairs. Don't forget, we can do this telepathically."

"Please try to get them upstairs fast, before anyone comes."

"Azalea, try to look angry. Say you are here for revenge."

"Viktoria, they're here. Get them to count to three and then throw in one of the balls filled with holy water."

*   *   *

"It's done. All that is left is some ashes. I'll continue with the siege; you clean up the ashes. Don't throw that just anywhere. Put it in this bag with the cross inside."

Greg peeked his head around the doorway. "I just heard the car pull into the driveway. Are you finished?"

"Almost. Go on ahead; open the door, so they will not think anything is strange."

I heard Greg running up the stairs and opening the door. The chatter of my children as they walked through the door caught my ears as I quickly cleaned up.

"We're home!" Cameron yelled.

"I'm starving!" Melisa said. "Come on, let's sit down and eat. Cameron, it's your turn to pray. Go on."

"Thank you, Lord, for the food and extra thanks for the ice cream Grandma Nelly bought. Amen."

"Thanks again, Nelly," I said as I walked into the dining room where they had already sat down, "for what you have done. It was a great help. I'm going to put a fresh pot of coffee on for dessert."

"No, honey," she said as she lightly touched my arm. "You don't need to; we bought coffee also." She pointed to a bag. She took a deep breath as she looked around the room. "I feel something different about the house. It looks brighter and smells so nice. It's not as dark as it was before."

"You are an angel, Nelly; thank you. I just changed the lightbulbs while everyone was out. I also opened the windows for some fresh air."

"Why didn't I think of that?" she asked herself. "Before it had such an odor; I don't smell it anymore."

We ate dinner as the kids played with each other. Once the coffee was consumed—and Cameron had eaten his ice cream—Nelly said, "Viktoria, I better leave. It's getting late."

"It was good to see you, Nelly," I said as I got up and gave her a hug. "God bless you."

"Viktoria, can you get my bag? I forgot it upstairs."

"When did you change your work bag?" I asked as I came down the stairs carrying her new bag. "I've never seen this one before. It's a very fancy one."

"Viktoria, that's not mine."

"Oh dear," I said looking down at the bag. "Brandon must have grabbed the wrong bag. Oh, Nelly, do you know what was happening when Brandon left? It's very unlike him not to take the right bag."

"You're right, but he dropped this on his way out," she said before handing me something.

"Why, I have never seen this before." I held it up to inspect it. "It's a black robe and has a symbol. I think I've seen this symbol before but where ..."

"Let me see that, Viktoria," Nelly commanded, holding out her hand. She looked at it for a long moment before announcing, "I think I have seen this robe before. It was my husband's; he was a member of some sort of club … I don't remember the name right now, but it was a gentlemen's club and there was that ring. I am surprised to see it; I thought his father had gotten rid of it."

"Maybe his father gave it to Brandon to keep as a keepsake, Nelly, but I've never seen Brandon wearing a ring before—apart from his wedding ring."

She looked around the room before looking back at me. She smiled. "You know, Viktoria, it's good to be here. I've missed this so much. We should get together more often."

"I agree," I said, lightly patting her hand. "You have not been in this house for a long time. Every time we planned for something, something else always came up. I'm so happy that you're here; I hope the kids don't tire you out; I know Cameron is a handful." I looked back at the kitchen. "Nelly, I'm making tea; would you like some?"

"Sure, if you still read the tea leaves," she said putting the bag down.

"Yes, I do. Why?"

"I just miss the days when we were able to sit down and chat."

I smiled as I remembered. "I have always wanted to talk to you but never really had a chance before. We will do it tonight, as soon as I get the tea ready."

"Thanks, Viktoria," she said and sat at the table in the kitchen. "Tea is nice, soothing. It relaxes me." She let out a yawn that she could not hide. "I feel so tired. I should go to bed soon, or I am going to park myself on this chair."

"Maybe we should reschedule your cup reading until tomorrow. Good night, Nelly. If you need me, I am going to be in my office working a bit longer."

"Don't read my cup without me," she said with a tired smile. She got up and headed to the guest room. "Good night."

"Good night, Nelly."

I headed up to my office, but I admit that my mind was racing.

I still could not get over the fact that Azalea and Lacey had seen Brandon. Maybe what they really saw was a jinn disguised as him; maybe that was the dark shadow we had all seen.

As this case got deeper, I was becoming more and more petrified. Perhaps I should back up from this case, not get as involved. I thought maybe Brandon was right; sometimes, things had to be left alone.

Once I was settled into my office, I noticed someone sitting in the chair. "I also think, Gabriellele, that I promised I would help and stop Lilith. And while this is far more than I bargained for, I cannot back away from the case. I gave my word, and I will do this."

"Thank you, Viktoria. I know you're scared; don't be. We're here for you as you are for us. Don't forget we have power as well; we won't let anyone hurt you or your family."

"Gabriellelc, how do you know all these things? Unless you can read my mind? … Can others … like you read too?"

"Yes, we all do; we can communicate among ourselves this way."

"Therefore, you could read other demons as well humans?"

"Only some. If they are ranked higher than us, we cannot read them."

"Can you do me a favor? Can you read Brandon's mind? Something is bothering me, and I need to know what's going on."

"What is it, Viktoria? What's bothering you?"

"It's about Azalea and Lacey. They both said they saw Brandon today."

"I don't know."

"You know what? As you said, it might be a jinn. It's possible."

"We cannot read jinn either. It's so hard; they're much faster than we are. … Maybe I am exaggerating again. I do have a tendency to do that." She tried to backtrack. "Just disregard what I said."

"I need to go over the files in case I missed something important. While I'm checking the files, you can keep me company and tell me more about yourself."

As I was checking over the files, Gabriellele was thinking about how we were going to find the rest of the people. "We don't know where they live, what their ages are, nothing at all."

Suddenly, I saw something. This never crossed my mind. Gabriellele was telling me about her birthdays from the past when it hit me. "It would help us a lot if their birthdays were the same."

We checked the rest of the files—an exact match.

Besides sharing the same birthday, Azalea and Carmella were born at the same time. That meant there were six hundred sixty-six born all over the world at the same time.

Then it hit me to look at the blood type. Bingo. All the same.

Also, all three were adopted. "I have to call Michael," I said, reaching for my phone. "I have to tell him what's going on."

# Chapter 5

## *Birthdays*

"Hi, Michael," I said to his voice mail. "I know it's one in the morning, and you can curse me out later, but I need to talk to you. It's very important; you know that I would never bother you unless it was big. Please call me."

A little while later, my phone rang. "Viktoria, I got your message. It had better be good, or you owe me big-time."

"As I said, it has to be big or I would not bother you at all. I was going over the files, and I noticed something: all three victims have some things in common. All their birthdays are the same, and they were all adopted."

"Listen, I'm going over to the office now. We can't wait for tomorrow. I don't have the files with me, so can you come in?"

"Yeah, I can leave the kids with their grandmother, Nelly. I'll meet you at the station. I don't want the kids to know anything about this case."

As I was driving to the station, Gabriellele gave me a warning. "There is someone with us. Are you sure you want to go over there?"

"Yes, Gabriellele, it's important. This concerns you and the others."

"Is this about what you were talking about with Michael? That we share the same birthdays?"

"Yes. We might also have come close to finding the rest of them. We might be able to save them faster than we think."

"Viktoria, soon I—and the others—will go to the light. Right now, I'm scared."

"You don't need to be scared," I said as I pulled into the station. "Okay, I have to go inside now; you can stay around if you want."

"I have an idea about how to find the rest before Lilith gets to them," was how Michael greeted me. "We have to be fast, though."

"What is it?" I said as I took off my coat.

"We have to check the hospital birth records for this date all over the United States."

"What about the rest of world? Don't forget, Michael, there are six hundred sixty-three females and one male left. Also the ones with us are adopted."

"How about the twins? Can we find them? Didn't you say that they hold the power close to hell? Far as I remember, weren't they born in New York State?"

"Michael, you are a genius! I'm going to call Greg, see if he can help us." I looked down at my ringing phone. "He's calling me now. Perfect timing!" I put it to my ear. "Hi, Greg, you must be eavesdropping. I was about to call you; Michael and I have a good lead in the case."

"Good thing I called then," Greg said. "I was concerned about you and the kids; is everything okay there? What were you saying about having a good lead?"

"Yes. I'm at the station now, and I know it's very late, but do you think you can come over?"

"Consider it done. I should be there in ten minutes."

"Okay," I said. After hanging up, I turned to Michael. "Greg is on his way. Let's start searching; when were they born?"

"They were born on February 14, 1982," he noted as he opened their files. "They are Valentine's Day babies."

"Are you sure? 1982? Michael, we have to check for all baby girls born that day and year."

A few minutes later, I heard the door open and looked up to see Greg walking in. "Look who's here," Michael said with a smile as he leaned back in his chair. "Our man! What did you do? Fly here?"

"If I say yes," Greg asked as he sat down, "would I get a ticket from you for speeding?"

Michael smirked. "Not this time."

"What have you found about the case? Are we getting close?"

"Well," Michael said, getting back to the files, "all three victims were born on the same day in the same year. All three were female, and all were adopted. Now we are searching for the birth records."

I looked at Greg. "What we need from you is a way to find the twins so they can help us to stop Lilith."

"When did you say they were born?"

"February 14, 1982."

Greg looked me in the eye. "Viktoria, are you okay with this?"

"Why would you ask that?" Michael asked, surprised. "Of course she is! She looks a little tired; that's all."

"I'm sorry, Michael; I suppose you don't know that Viktoria lost twins at birth. They had the same birthday too."

Michael looked at me. "I'm so sorry, Viktoria. I didn't know. This must be very hard for you, especially with this case."

"It was a long time ago," I said, wishing Greg hadn't brought this up. "Brandon and I were only engaged; I was still in college. Brandon had a new job in the hospital actually. I think the Lawson firm found him just about the time I found out I was pregnant. We were ecstatic. We got married before the twins were due.

"However, during the birth, the umbilical cord was wrapped around one of the babies' necks, and he was a stillborn. The other baby died the next day. I saw the first baby for few seconds and the other baby the next morning. He was in an incubator when I left him, but right after I came up to my room, the nurse told us they had lost him. Since then, I have tried to block it away."

"Since you are psychic, have you ever seen them or felt their presence in the last twenty-seven years?"

"You know what, Michael? I suppose that since I tried to block it so hard, I did not see them or hear them at all. I have never talked about this with anyone until today. The kids don't know anything about their twin brothers. I did not want to get hurt again or hurt them by telling them." I sighed before looking around the room. My eyes landed on the files. I clapped my hands once. "Come on, guys! Let's get back to work. It's three in the morning. We need these addresses, so can you make a few copies?" I said passing some files to Michael.

"Look at this, Viktoria," Michael said, coming closer to me. "Of all the birth registrations in the state of New York, there were one hundred forty-five girls and thirty-two boys, one set of twins. The twins were born on Long Island in a general hospital, and there was another baby boy born as a stillborn at the same as time as the twins.

"What I am saying is that there was only one set of twins born that night in all of New York."

"Long Island General Hospital?" I asked. "But I had my twins there that night too. It should show their registration as well. However, there is nothing about a second set of twins."

"That's what I'm saying; why doesn't it show that?"

"I just remembered what you said, Greg, about when Leila switched the boys. She must have then erased some files. Maybe, accidentally, she erased my twins' files too. That could have happened, right?"

"Greg, we have to check the death registrations in that hospital that night. How many babies were stillborns?"

"That night shows two stillborns. One was a boy and one a girl. Their birth records have no names. There is no record showing anything about the birth of your twin boys or any kind of record showing that you were even admitted to the hospital that night. There is no death of any babies the next day either. It was not registered from Long Island General Hospital. Maybe you're right; they must have been erased accidentally."

"That's impossible. Michael, I think we're confusing ourselves; we need a break. Let's get some coffee."

"At least they show that only one baby boy lived. So how do we get the address?" Michael asked.

"The address is shown on the register as being in upstate New York. We get the names and address there," I said.

"Viktoria, I'll do it. I know what to do from here; let me get into the system."

"Look at this, they only lived there for few years and then they moved," Michael said.

"Is there any forwarding address?" I asked.

"Let me see ... no, there isn't one. But don't worry, we can still get it. We have to check any kind of records like licenses or unpaid traffic tickets. There must be something. We could also check their tax returns."

"Look," I said, "I can't stay that long; I have to go back home. I am extremely tired, and I need to get the kids to school in the morning. So that is it from me, but if you find anything, let me know. Good night." I got up to leave.

"We all should get some rest," Greg said. "Michael, we can continue with this later. We're coming, Viktoria! Wait!"

"Greg, call Viktoria back here," I heard Michael say, "I think I have the address."

"Viktoria!" I heard Greg yell. I turned around. "Come back! Michael has something to show you!"

"Okay, I'm coming. This better be good," I mumbled. I was so tired all I could think about was my nice, warm bed.

"Greg, write this phone number down," Michael instructed. "And this is the address. We can go over tomorrow and ask around. Viktoria," he said when he saw me, "we have a phone number and an address. We are checking on the baby now." Michael then proceeded to talk into a phone.

"Who is Michael talking to, Greg?"

"He is talking to his friend Den from the FBI. He's looking for more information on this family."

"Okay, Den," Michael said into his phone. "What was the kid's name?" He wrote something down. "Okay, got it. Thanks for the info; I appreciate it." He put the phone down and grinned at Greg and me. "I am the man! I have some information; it's bad, but it's still information."

"What is the bad information?"

"Well, we know that the kid's name was Alvin."

"What happened to him?" I asked.

"Unfortunately, the kid passed away from meningitis in high school. After his death, the family returned to Italy. They couldn't stay here any longer."

"What is the other news, Michael?"

"Viktoria, his mother took it the worst, but because of her illness, they're back. They came a few weeks ago. They live in Locust Valley, New York."

"It's something, Michael. It's the best news ever. We're getting closer to this, I can feel it!"

"Viktoria, I don't think you heard me right: the kid died. He does not exist anymore."

"I heard you, but this kid is not dead. They set this up, switching names with someone who died from meningitis. I am telling you, he is alive! We will find him! You even said it yourself, Greg; they have been touched by Leila, and they are immortal! He is protected by angels!"

"Let's go and celebrate this news," Greg said. "What do you guys say? Come on; we need to eat first. How about it? I also need a hell of a cup of strong coffee to wake me up."

"That's an excellent idea," I said with a smile. "I will pick up something for the kids."

Greg and I went to Dunkin' Donuts, which was open all night. After we all got large coffees—and I got some doughnuts for the kids—we headed back.

"Thanks, guys, for my coffee and breakfast. I have to get my kids ready for school, so I'm going back home. See you all later!" I waved good-bye.

"Michael," I heard Greg whisper, "I'm worried about Viktoria. I sense or have a bad feeling that something is following her. Also that something is draining her energy."

"Do you think so? I thought it was just that she is tired."

"I've known Viktoria for a long time, and this is not her. She's usually very hyperactive."

"This case has worn her out; we should keep an eye on her."

"Michael, you also could use a siege in your house. Carry this holy water with you at all times. You might need it, because you also got involved with this entity."

"Thanks, Greg. I will do that siege and holy water thing. I'll see you later then."

# Chapter 6

## *Grandma Nelly*

*Thank God I'm home!* I thought to myself as I closed the front door to my house. *Everyone is sleeping; I should get myself into bed also.*

"Oh my, dear, do you always work this late?" I heard someone ask as I was about to go up the stairs.

I turned around and walked to the kitchen where I saw Grandma Nelly sitting with a cup of something steaming in front of her. "I didn't know you were up, Nelly. I'm so sorry if I woke you."

"No, honey," she said with a shake of her head. "Just couldn't sleep for some reason. I also wanted to talk to you; I've wanted to do this for the longest time, but I was not brave enough. I didn't know how you would react."

"What do you mean, how I would react?" I asked, sitting down across from her.

"You don't look well; let me make you a cup of hot chocolate, then we can talk about this." She put some water on to boil and grabbed a mug. "It started to worry me a while ago … something I overheard. At first, I could not believe it, and then I started to look for evidence. I searched, and I found out it's true."

"Is everything all right, Nelly? Did something happen?"

"Everything's okay; nothing happened. The kids are fine. I wanted to tell you what I know; it's very important, and I cannot keep it secret anymore."

"What is it? What did you overhear that has been bothering

you this much? I have never seen you this upset, Nelly. You look like you're shaking. Are you all right? You don't look well."

She closed her eyes and clutched her chest. "Viktoria, my heart medicine ... get it! It's in my bag!"

I ran to her bag and almost ripped it open. I found the pills and ran back to her; I put two in her hand and said, "Okay, right now, take this and the water. I'm calling an ambulance."

My hands shook as I dialed the number, but finally I got through. After the operator asked how he could help me, I said, "I need an ambulance! My mother-in-law might be having a heart attack!"

The person asked for my address, which I gave, and said an ambulance would be there as quickly as possible.

I went back to my mother-in-law. "How do you feel now, Nelly?" I asked as I took her hand.

"Viktoria, I have to tell you something. I can't keep it to myself anymore. It's about what I know about the twins."

"Not now, Nelly," I said as my face became covered in blue and red lights. "Don't talk; you need rest. Look, the ambulance is here."

"We're taking her to Long Island General Hospital," one EMT told me as they loaded her into the van.

"I'll follow you."

"Mom," I saw Melisa come out. "What is ... what is wrong? What happened to Grandma Nelly?"

"Melisa, Grandma Nelly had a heart attack. She'll be okay. They're taking her to the hospital now. No one is going to school. Today, stay home and watch your siblings. I'll call you when I have more information."

"How about Dad?" she asked as I grabbed my purse and keys. "Is he coming back?"

"I'll call your father. If he calls before that, ask him to call me. Don't tell him anything."

*Oh my god, what a night!* I couldn't help but think as I got into the car and drove to the hospital. I hoped she would be all right. "Please, God, let her be all right."

I needed to call Brandon and tell him about his mom. I dialed the number and hooked up my hands-free set. "Brandon," I said after he picked up, "you have to come back as soon as possible. It's your mom."

"What happened to Mom?" he asked, frightened.

"She had a heart attack. An ambulance took her to Long Island General Hospital; I'm following them. You need to be there."

"Did she have any problems with her heart before?"

"She must have, because she asked for her medicine from her bag."

"Look, Viktoria, I'm on my way. I have a friend who is a doctor in that hospital; I will ask him to go over there and take care of her. Don't worry."

"Who is the doctor?"

"I don't know if you remember Doctor Justin; he is the best in the field."

"Yes, I do, I do remember him. His daughter went missing, right?"

"Yes. Viktoria, when you get there, ask for him. He will help you with Mom. Call me back."

*I hope she's okay,* I thought as I pulled into the parking lot. *God, I feel so bad! She wanted to talk to me and say something. It seemed important to her. Please, God, let her be okay!*

"Melisa," I said into the phone as I sat in the car. I had decided to call home before going into the hospital; they probably wouldn't tell me anything new for hours anyway. "Hi, baby. Just called to say we're here now. They took her in, so I don't know what's going on. I'm going to shut off my phone, so please call your dad and tell him they took Grandma Nelly inside to do an operation on her."

"Mom, she's all right, right? She will make it, right?"

"I hope so, baby. Let's all pray for her; that will help her."

"Okay, Mom. Bye for now."

"I will call you if there are changes. Don't forget to call your father."

I hung up and walked into the lobby. I walked over to the desk and asked, "Excuse me, is Doctor Justin here? I have to see him."

"He's here, but he went into an emergency operation."

I let out a sigh of relief. "Okay then. My name is Viktoria. I am the patient's daughter-in-law. I will be waiting for him here."

"Sure, I'll tell him," the nurse said. I smiled before going to sit on one of the hard chairs.

It was cold in the waiting room. I'd never liked them much—the walls were painted white with a strip of color here and there, and people were just sitting there on cold plastic chairs with worried faces waiting for loved ones. It was going to be a long day.

"Hi, Lacey," I said into my phone an hour later. They were still in the operating room. "Is that you?"

"Yes, Mom. How is Grandma Nelly doing? Is she okay now?"

"I don't know. It's been an hour since they took her into the operating room, and she's not out yet. Did your dad call?"

"Yes, Mom. He said he's just getting his car from the parking lot and should be there soon."

"How are Cameron and Melisa? What are they doing?"

"They're fine. Mom, Michael is on the other line. Let me answer the phone."

"Go ahead, honey. Tell him what happened. I have to hang up now too. I'm going inside; I'll call you back in an hour."

\*    \*    \*

"Michael, Mom is not here. Grandma Nelly had a heart attack, and they took her to the hospital in an ambulance."

"Yes, I know. I have spoken to your mom already. Are you guys okay?"

"Mom said they are operating on her now."

"Then call me if you need anything, Lacey."

"Michael, are you going to the hospital?"

"Yes. Do you kids want to come with me?"

"Thanks, but we have to stay here."

Michael hung up and leaned back in his chair. *Why didn't she mention the twins?* he wondered. *I cannot get that out of my mind. She looked so hurt—and scared. It keeps playing in my head.* He tapped his foot. *Sitting and waiting in suspense is killing me. I'm so worried about her mother-in-law, Nelly. I hope Brandon gets there in time.*

\*   \*   \*

Back in the hospital, I waited with my hands clasped tightly together on my lap. What would I say if he asked me how this happened? I couldn't help but think. What would I say? I could not mention the twins to him; he would get angry. I knew it hurt him so much every time someone mentioned them.

Out of nowhere, I heard Azalea. "Viktoria, don't worry. She's okay. Look, her doctor is coming over to you now."

I looked up, and sure enough, the doctor was right there. "Doctor Justin, I'm so glad you're here."

"I'm happy to help. As soon as Brandon told me what had happened, I told him not to worry, and I came here."

"How is Nelly?"

"She's fine. Her heart is doing well, except ..." His voice trailed off.

"What happened?"

"She had a stroke during the operation; she might have some speech problems and little to no vision in her left eye. We can't do much until she comes to. She's in recovery now."

"We all love Grandma Nelly," I said, terrified and relieved at the same time. I started babbling, since I didn't know what else to do. "She is like a mother to me; we called her an archangel without wings. She was always very helpful to everyone; she was always there for us. Thank God she's okay!"

"I'm sure she'll be fine; we'll take good care of her."

I saw the doctor look over my shoulder. I turned around, wondering what he was looking at, and noticed my husband.

"Brandon! I'm glad you're here; Doctor Justin was just telling me about the operation."

"How did the operation go, Justin? How is she doing?"

"As I was just telling Viktoria, your mom is fine. However, during the operation, she had a stroke, so we don't know how that affected her. She may have a speech problem, or she may not feel her left side. She might need another operation later. We'll have to wait and see."

"Can we see her?"

"Not yet; she's in the recovery room. Don't worry; when she goes to her room, I will call you."

"Thanks so much for your help," Brandon said before shaking the doctor's hand. Doctor Justin nodded and walked away.

"Brandon, it was so strange. There was nothing wrong with her; it was early in the morning. I had just come from the office."

"What were you doing so late in the office?"

"What happened was, after everyone went to bed, I decided to go over the files to see if I could see something that we might have missed before. Then I called Michael, so we met in the office to go over the files more carefully.

"When I came home, she was up, waiting. I asked her if she was okay, and she said that she was. Then she said we needed to talk, and she wanted to talk to me about something that had happened a long time ago. Then her face started changing color, and she asked me to get her heart medication from her bag. Then I called the ambulance."

"What would be so important that she wanted to talk to you so badly about it? Did she say anything?"

"The only thing she mentioned is that there was something she overheard and I needed to know. Whatever it is, we'll find out when she gets better; I'm sure she will tell us."

"Main thing is her getting better. She has the best doctors in the world."

I nodded in agreement. "I'm going outside to call the kids. They must be worried. I'll meet you upstairs."

He nodded and headed for the elevators as I went outside. I dialed the number and waited for someone to pick up.

"Mom," Melisa asked, breathless. "How is Grandma Nelly doing? Is she still in the operation?"

"She's fine; the operation went well. Don't worry. Your dad is here too. I should be home this afternoon. Dad sends his love. Please take care of your brother and sister."

She told me that she would before hanging up. I was about to go inside when I heard, "Viktoria, wait for me!"

I turned around. "I cannot believe you, Michael! What are you doing here? I would have called you!"

"I know that, but I didn't want to leave you and Brandon alone at a time like this."

"Thank you for your concern; you're a good friend. Michael, if you want to go see Brandon, he's upstairs in the waiting room. I'll join you as soon as I call Greg and tell him what's going on."

"You don't need to call him."

"You told him, didn't you?"

He nodded. "He said he would stop by your house and drop off breakfast for the kids. Then he would come here."

I couldn't help but smile. "What would we do without you both?"

Michael and I decided to wait for Greg. Once he showed up, we went upstairs. "Honey," I said when we got upstairs, "look at who I found! These two guys downstairs were looking for us." Brandon greeted the two guys. "Any news on Grandma Nelly?"

"No, not yet. The nurse came in and said that she's still in the recovery room. As soon as she wakes up, the nurse will call us."

"Look," I said glancing out the door. "Doctor Justin is coming with someone. I hope it's not bad news."

"Don't panic!" the doctor greeted us with a smile. "This is not bad news. We took her to her room; you can see her in twenty minutes. I just wanted to introduce you to my assistant, Doctor Damien Amore. He's the best assistant, in case Nelly needs a second operation."

"Thank you, Lord," I said to the ceiling before looking back at the doctors. "I am so relived that she's okay. Did she wake up yet?"

"Not yet. When you go inside, don't let her talk—even if she tries to. We don't want her to tire herself out. Also try not to look worried; it might upset her more."

"Whatever you say, Justin," Brandon said. "Long as Mom is okay. By the way, it was nice to meet you, Doctor Damien. I'm happy to see that my mother is in safe hands."

"Please, if you have any questions, don't hesitate to ask. I will be happy to answer any for you."

"Thank you for your great care, Doctor Damien," I said. "It was a pleasure to meet you."

"I suppose you can go to see Nelly now for a few minutes," said Doctor Justin.

"I don't know what to expect," I said when the doctors left. "I hope with all my heart that she is okay."

We went to her room and saw her lying there so peacefully. I wished I had a magic wand so that I could make her better. It hurt me to see her like that.

"Brandon," I said, trying to look at him, but losing that battle. "I need to go out. I don't feel good. I have never seen her like this; I cannot stay. I'll be back."

I walked out the door and saw Michael and Greg standing there. "Viktoria, how is Nelly doing?"

"She is sleeping like an angel. I hope she's not in pain."

"No, I don't think so," Greg said. "Don't worry; she's a strong woman. She'll be just fine."

"I don't know what I would tell the kids if anything happened to her. They'd be so badly hurt. They love their grandma Nelly."

"Doctor Damien is coming," Michael said. "Maybe he has some good news."

"Doctor Damien," I said when he was close enough to us, "I'm praying for good news, hoping that she will be okay."

"I am here to tell you that there was nothing but good news on all the tests. She will not need an operation after all. She will just need a little speech therapy."

"Thank God! That is wonderful news! I have to go to upstairs to tell Brandon right away!"

"Okay then, let's go. We can tell him the good news together. I believe Doctor Justin will be joining us in a few minutes."

"There's Brandon over there. And Doctor Justin too."

"Hi, Damien. I suppose you already told them."

"Yes, I told Viktoria but not her husband yet. We thought we would tell him together."

"Nelly is doing better than we expected." Brandon and I looked at each other, and we couldn't stop the smiles from growing. "I heard so much about her from Doctor Justin. He told me that she is a wonderful person. I have to go now, but I wish the family good luck."

"Brandon, are you okay? Your face looks white, like you have seen a ghost."

"Viktoria, does Doctor Damien look familiar to you? I feel that we have seen him somewhere before, but I cannot not put my finger on where."

"I don't know. I don't see anyone except Grandma Nelly. I need a couple of days to relax. I need to get Nelly's room ready at home for when she's out of the hospital. We can't leave her by herself. She needs to be taken care of."

"Sure, Viktoria," Michael said. "Take off as much time as you need. Greg and I will work on the case to see what else we can find out. We're leaving now, but call us if we are needed. Give our love to Grandma Nelly; we are praying for her."

"I don't know how to express gratitude to you guys for your help. I'm glad you both were here with us." I kissed them both on the cheek before leaning back. "I'm going upstairs to see Nelly. See you both later. Bye."

As I was walking upstairs, I heard Azalea's voice. She sounded like she was happy, but for some reason, I could not see her. However, I could hear her talking to someone; I started to wonder about that. I knew it was not Gabriellele because she was with me. When I walked into Grandma Nelly's room, I overheard Azalea talking to Nelly.

"Grandma Nelly, you have to wake up and get better. Your grandkids and Viktoria need you, especially now."

"Azalea, I see you are keeping Nelly company. It's nice of you to tell her that we need her."

"Nelly was mumbling your name before, and I just wanted to respond to her, so that she did not feel like she was alone. Also being an ex-medical intern, I felt I had to be here next to her."

"I left her with Brandon. Where is he? Have you seen him?"

"No, I haven't. When I got here, he was not around, and then I heard Nelly calling you. When I started talking to her, she kept saying she was sorry for all this."

"Well, did she say anything else? What would that be, Azalea? Did she make herself sick just to tell me something? I'm glad Brandon was not here; he would've kept asking what it was. I would not know what to tell him, and even if I did tell him the truth, he probably wouldn't believe me."

"That young doctor came in and held her hands tight, and then he hugged her. He said, 'You are going to be just fine.' Did she know him?"

"Not that I know of, but she has a face that reminds everyone of their mother or grandmother. She's an angel; everyone loves her. She probably reminded him of someone he knew. That's normal, because she always did."

The door opened, and Brandon walked in. "I was looking for you, Viktoria. When did you get here? Did she wake up?"

"I just got here, but she is still sleeping. Brandon, I need to go home, take care of a couple of things, and bring the kids over."

"Melisa is on her way with the kids. I just spoke to her a few minutes ago. I told them they could see her."

I nodded. "That's excellent, Brandon. Can you go downstairs and get me a cup of coffee? I really need one. Also get something to snack on. I feel a bit lightheaded; I think my blood sugar is down."

"I need to see Justin too before he goes home. Let's see if there is anything new with her condition."

"That's a good idea," I said, trying anything to get him out of the room. "Go."

Doctor Damien walked in to see how Grandma Nelly was doing, just as Brandon was about to step out.

"You haven't left yet?" Brandon said.

"No, not yet. I have a family member who is sick over here too. I went to see her."

"I'm sorry to hear that. I hope she is okay."

"It's my mother; she has a terminal illness. We cannot do much, just make her comfortable and pain free."

"My heart goes out to you, Dr. Damien," I said. "I'm so sorry. I didn't mean to upset you."

"I stopped by earlier to check on her. She was mumbling, and I came to see if she was awake yet, but I see she is not."

"Viktoria, you can talk to her. She can probably hear you. It might just be that she is tired; she should wake up soon."

Someone knocked on the door before opening it. "Mom?" Melisa asked as she walked in. "Can we come in? We want to see Grandma Nelly. Has she woken up yet? Can we talk to her?"

"Come in, Melisa. Take a deep breath. No, she has not woken up yet. Doctor Damien and I were just discussing it."

"Sorry, Mom, I didn't mean to interrupt anything. Go ahead and discuss whatever you want to. We'll wait outside."

"Wait. Let me introduce you to Doctor Damien. He is your father's friend Doctor Justin's assistant, and he is in charge of Grandma Nelly while she is under their care."

"It is my pleasure to meet you, Doctor Damien," Melisa said as she shook his hand.

"The pleasure is all mine."

Cameron walked into the room. I could see that Lacey was trying to hold him back, but he walked right in. "How about us, Doctor Damien? Aren't you happy to meet us also?"

"Who is this young man?" the doctor asked with a smile.

I stepped forward. "Well, this young man is Cameron. He's my son, who likes to stick his nose in situations where it doesn't belong."

Doctor Damien laughed. "Well, Cameron, it's my pleasure to meet such a smart young man as you."

"Mine too!" Cameron said, giving him a smile. "And this is my sister, Lacey. She does not like to talk that much; she's shy."

"It's nice to meet the shy Lacey too."

"Let's not keep Doctor Damien from his other patients," I said.

"I'll stop by before I leave to check up on Grandma Nelly," the doctor said.

"Why? Is Grandma Nelly your grandma too?" Cameron asked.

The doctor laughed and shook his head. "No, Cameron, she is not. But I do care for her as if she were my grandma."

"Well, I suppose you can call her Grandma Nelly too. It's okay with me."

"Thank you, Cameron. I'll remember that." Doctor Damien looked at us before saying, "I'll see you later then." Then he left.

"Oh my God, Mom!" Melisa squealed once the door was closed. "Why didn't you call me before and tell me how handsome he is? I hope he is still here when I'm doing my internship over here at the end of the year!"

"Mom, look," Lacey said, "and listen! Grandma Nelly is saying something!"

"What is it, Lacey?" I tried to hear, but Melisa's gushing was not helping. "Hush, Melisa; I cannot hear what Lacey is trying to say."

"Mom! Grandma Nelly is awake! She's asking for you!"

I rushed to her bedside. "Yes, Nelly, I am here. We are all here."

"Viktoria," Nelly whispered. The left side of her mouth couldn't open as much as the right side. "I need to tell you something."

"I know, Nelly, I know," I said as I patted her hand. "Just not now. Whatever it is, it can wait. We have to concentrate on your well-being; you have to get some rest." I looked up at my eldest daughter. "Melisa, go get your father and tell him Grandma Nelly is awake."

"Wait, Melisa," Nelly said a little louder. "I need to talk to your mom first. Alone."

I ignored her. "Melisa, go get your father and Doctor Justin here now." I turned back to the woman in the bed. "Grandma Nelly, as I have told you before, I do not want to hear anything from you until you are feeling much better."

A few minutes later, Brandon came running in with Doctor Justin behind him. "Mom! How are you doing? You gave us quite a scare! How do you feel now? Look, Mom, look at who is here with us: Doctor Justin! You do remember him, right?"

"Brandon, calm down. Yes, I feel much better. I do remember Doctor Justin; he always stopped by to see how I was doing. Brandon, I got sick, not senile."

"I can tell you're feeling much better." He turned and looked at Doctor Justin. "I'll talk to you, Justin, about this. You've never mentioned that Mom was your patient before."

"Main thing, Grandma Nelly," I said, "is that you're feeling much better. So, Justin, when can we take her home?"

"She has to stay for a few days, just so we can observe her under our care. Maybe this coming Friday she'll be free to go home. We'll get full home care for her. She cannot be alone and has to have a nurse coming in for a while."

"All right then. We can get the room ready for Grandma Nelly and have a nurse come to our house."

"No, dear," Nelly said. "I want to go home. I'll be fine. You heard Justin; there will be a nurse and a full home-care service will be coming. I don't want to be a burden on you; I'll be just fine."

"Nelly, I will not take 'No' for an answer. You are coming to our house on Friday. I will be very hurt if you choose not to, so are we agreed on that?"

"Well, if you say so, Viktoria. By the way, you owe me a tea leaf reading. Don't forget."

"You know what, Grandma Nelly?" Melisa asked. "I'll help Mom to make the tea."

"Right after that, we will have an ice cream cake. Mommy makes the best ice cream cake!" Cameron announced.

"That would be an excellent idea. I have not had your mom's ice cream cake for the longest time, Cameron."

"So, we're all set. Okay, guys, we need to leave Grandma Nelly to rest. That's enough for today; I want everybody to go home. I'll see you all tomorrow after school. Okay, everyone?"

"Mom, I want to stay with Grandma Nelly tonight and keep her company," Melisa said. "Plus, I need to study for my exam tomorrow tonight, and I can find some quiet here. You can go home."

"Well, if you're sure, you can stay and keep her company, as long as you do not get Grandma tired. As soon as she falls asleep, you can study. You're coming home tomorrow morning though."

"I will go straight to school from here, because I have an eight o'clock class and my test is at nine."

"Okay then, Melisa, I'll see you tomorrow night." I turned to my mother-in-law. "And, Nelly, I will see you tomorrow morning. Get some rest, and I hope you feel better today. Melisa, do not forget what I told you; do not get your grandma tired."

# Chapter 7

## *Help from Babushka*

"Gabriellele, I think I'm sensing the presence of my dad." I looked around. "Babushka, is that you?"

"Yes, baby, I need to speak to you. It's starting to get dangerous; I must tell you something."

"Babushka, if you're going to ask me to stop with this Lilith thing, please don't, because you know that I can't. Plus, Grandma Nelly had a heart attack and had an operation. She has to stay in the hospital until next Friday. I'm so tired of this case; it's getting me frustrated, and I want to stop it!"

"I know, baby, but I am worried about … we decided that you and everyone around you needs protection so there will be two jinns that will protect you. They obey you and only you. Their names are Shia and Zanah. They both have the power to appear as humans and vanish like demons, so do not be afraid of them. They are here to help you."

"Babushka, I know that you know something about this case … more than you are letting on. What was Nelly going to tell me that was so important? She got sick, but did something hurt her or did a demon do something to stop her from telling me? This is why you are giving us protection, right?"

"You have to listen to Nelly; do not judge her when she tells you. Don't say anything to hurt her feelings; you have to promise me that. Also, baby, do not jump to any conclusions either."

"Okay, I promise, Babushka; I will not say anything to her that might hurt her. I know she would never hurt me—or anyone else—so do not worry about that."

"Can you tell me something? When you said I need jinn to protect me, you said *we* decided it. Who is we? Did you mean … are my twins and Mom … are they with you?"

"No, baby, when I said that I meant the elders and Leila, the birth angel. They are the ones sending you these good jinn."

"Babushka, instead of sending me the jinn, why doesn't Leila stop Lilith from getting the twins? Leila and Quelamia gave them the power to close the door to hell. I am sure they can stop it. Alternatively, tell me, where are the twins? Will we find them before anyone else dies?"

"Baby, it's not as easy as it sounds. Leila and Quelamia cannot be seen by anyone, including Lilith. This has to be done by others like you."

"Why?"

"Because it would start a war between the angels."

"Babushka, how would I be able to communicate with them? And if they have the power to appear as humans, how would I know?"

"As a human, always check the eyes. They will talk to you with their eyes. You can see them and communicate with them telepathically. They obey only you."

"What happens if they do not obey me and turn against me?"

"Viktoria, remind them God placed them to obey; otherwise, they will go back to hell."

"Thank you so much, Babushka. I knew I could count on you and Mom. I love you both."

"One day, we need to talk about the twins; it's important."

"Babushka, they are next to you. When you crossed over, they were there. Did you see my babies? Why don't I ever feel their presence? Every time I asked Mom, she always said they were angels and they needed to do their jobs of helping others. She never gave me a straight answer. If they are not there to hear me, tell them I love them; I miss them with all my heart."

"We'll talk about the twins later. I'm sure they know that. Viktoria, stay safe and do not forget what I have told you. And do not worry about Nelly; she will be just fine as long as you keep an eye on her. May the angels watch over you. I am losing my energy, but I will be back."

I turned back to the other person I was talking to. "It must be my lucky day; everyone wants to talk to me, but something always happens before they can tell me whatever it is. The suspense is killing me! Gabriellele, do you know anything about this that you're not telling?"

"Viktoria, there is something we cannot tell you because it has to be told by Nelly. What I mean is, sometimes something has to be lived and appreciated to make life better."

"You're right, Gabriellele. I do not know what I will do when you see the light and leave me. I will miss you and Azalea."

"We will be assigned to other projects, so we will see each other. You're forgetting that you're a psychic! Most likely, we will see each other again."

"Where is Azalea? I don't see her around."

"Azalea stayed behind at the hospital; she is watching over Nelly and Melisa. I'm sure she has missed being in a hospital surrounding."

"We are here, Gabriellele. I don't know when this nightmare is going to stop or how it's going to end, but the one thing I do know is that I don't want anyone else getting hurt. Another thing I want to know is, is Brandon worrying about me? He will not stop asking if his mother said anything. That makes me think that he is hiding something from me. I hope he's not hiding anything; he knows better than that."

"I don't see Brandon's car in the driveway," I said when I peeked out of the living room window. "He has the kids with him, so he should have been here before me. I hope nothing happened to them;

I can't take any more trips to the hospital. I'll call him to find out." I dialed his number and waited for him to pick up. "Brandon, where are you? I just got home, and I did not see the car. Is everything okay? Are the kids okay?"

"Don't panic. You're overreacting again. We are all fine; we stopped to get something to eat, and we will be leaving for home soon."

"With everything that has been happening lately, you can't blame me for getting worried over nothing. We've had enough excitement to last for years."

"Whose fault is that, Viktoria? I told you before, don't get involved with this. It sounded dangerous the day you ended up in the hospital, if you forgot. Did Mom say anything to you yet?"

"Not yet. I told her that whatever it is, I don't want to know because her health worries me. She gets too excited and nervous. I don't want to know. By the way, why is this bothering you? It almost seems like you are hiding something and you don't want me to find out about it.

"Brandon, whatever it is, we'll both find out, I promise you. I will ask your mother to tell us when we're both there if that is okay with you, so let's not argue over this now."

He sighed. "We should be home soon; do you need anything?"

"Yes, pick up milk."

We both said good-bye and hung up. Gabriellele then asked me, "Viktoria, what are you going to do? About Alvin, I mean. How can you be sure that he is not dead? What happens if it is not him? What will we do then?"

"You know what, Gabriellele? If those twins were given powers, that also means they are almost immortal. Somehow, Alvin's soul was moved by something. The only thing I can think of at the moment is that they switched bodies with another dead person. You know, Gabriellele, just remember what Michael told me today about Doctor Damien."

"What about him?"

"Michael said that Doctor Damien reminded him of someone, but at the moment, I could not see it but I think I know now."

"Who does he remind you of?"

"You. And he also reminds me of Brandon when he was young—his body posture, the way he moves his mouth when he talks. And a bit of my babushka—kind, loving, and caring. Did you see him?"

"No, I have not seen him yet. That was Azalea."

I nod. "Right. But I felt something about him. He is such a caring person; he is so easygoing, but I feel bad for him. His mother is not doing well, he said. I think Doctor Justin is very lucky to have an assistant like him."

"Brandon is here, Viktoria."

"Okay, Gabriellele, I want you to go to the back room. If you feel uncomfortable, go to Lacey's room; she likes to talk to you. She feels very important when she sees you around."

"Mom," Cameron said as he came in holding a bag. "We bought an ice cream cake and some fruit so we could have some fruit salad. We also bought some whipped cream! It's chocolate; you like chocolate, right, Mom?"

"Of course, Cameron. How can I say no to you as long as you don't overdo it? As soon as you're done, you need to go to bed, okay? It's getting late."

"Mom, can I stay home tomorrow? I want to come with you to see Grandma Nelly!"

"No, baby, but you can stay home the day Grandma Nelly comes home from the hospital. That's a promise."

"Hooray! Is she coming to our house?"

"Yes, baby. We'll go together and pick her up. How is that?"

"It's an excellent idea. Is Dad coming with us too?"

"You bet I am. And we can stop by the ice cream parlor and buy your grandma's favorite ice cream!"

"Yes! We are going to celebrate, right, Dad?"

"If you do not go to bed right now, we will just rethink that."

"Consider me in bed right now! Hold on a second, I have to have my fruit salad ice cream first."

"Viktoria." Brandon turned to me as our son dug into his ice cream like it was going out of style. "Did you find out anything about Mom?"

"No, not yet. But I'll send a text message to Melisa." I took out my phone and texted: "How is Grandma doing?"

*Why didn't I think of that before?* I wondered, and then I felt my phone vibrating in my hand. "Oh, she's calling. Hi, Melisa, how is Grandma Nelly doing?"

"Oh, she has just fallen asleep. I'm downstairs getting a snack. Doctor Damien is here too. We were having coffee together, but as soon as I am done, I'm going upstairs, so don't worry, Mom. She is fine."

"Just call to let us know if anything changes."

"Okay."

"Good luck with your test tomorrow. And Daddy says not to stay up too late."

"Okay, Mom. I have to go now."

"Viktoria," Brandon said when I hung up the phone, "we need to talk about your work. This is getting in the way, and that is starting to cause problems. You have to stop this or pass it to someone else. Greg can take over this case. I don't want you to proceed any further."

"You can't be serious, Brandon. How you can ask me that? You know better! Once I have taken a case—and I have been on this case a few months—I just can't pass it over to someone else! It doesn't work like that, and you know it! I have a responsibility to be there for other people; they rely on me!"

"What responsibility? To whom? The dead people? They are dead! They are gone! Done with this life! There is nothing you can do!"

"I don't know what the hell is wrong with you, Brandon! Before I started working with this psychic case, you were the one who kept pushing me to work and get myself some confidence! Now you're telling me to stop! I know this is not you talking; I am brushing aside everything you are telling me. Let it go. Since I'm not dropping this case or passing it to any other psychic, don't ever broach this topic again, do you understand me? Now I am going to my office to work. If you still have a problem, you had better deal with it fast."

"Viktoria, you are being unreasonable and acting like a child right now. Think about what I am saying. I am not telling you to leave your job, only this case!"

"Brandon, read my lips: N-O!"

I ran upstairs to our bedroom, slammed the door, and began pacing.

"Viktoria," I heard Gabriellele ask, "is Brandon okay? I heard what he said. Do you think he is right? I have never seen him so mad."

"You know, Gabriellele, he thinks you and the other dead ... that there is nothing I can do to help you or the others. He does not want to understand! Do you think you should show yourself to him? Then we will see what he thinks. Go down; he is in his office. Go ahead and show yourself to him!"

"Are you sure?" Gabriellele asked, concerned.

"I've told you before, I am sure. Go ahead and show yourself." I felt another presence. "Good timing, Azalea. Gabriellele's about to show herself to Brandon. Would you like to show yourself to him too?"

"Viktoria, don't you think you are overreacting? What happens if he gets scared or ... I don't know."

"Azalea, honey, don't worry. He thinks that when people die, we cannot help them with anything, that they are gone. Done. So if it is as easy as he says, he should not be afraid of a spirit. Go ahead, go. I will be coming downstairs with pleasure as soon as he yells my name."

"Let's do it then," Azalea said.

"Azalea, you go through the door; I'll go through the wall," Gabriellele told her.

"I hope he doesn't have a heart attack."

"Azalea, don't say anything. Let's watch him first; let's wait and see how he responds to us being there."

"Viktoria," I heard Gabriellele whisper, "we're here. He's going over his files."

"Okay then, move something so that you can get his attention. Otherwise, he will not take his eyes off those files."

"Okay, let's move the file next to Azalea." They became silent. "Not responding. Let's flick the light, okay, Azalea?"

"What the hell is going on with this light?" I heard Brandon yell. "I just changed it the other day! And I don't even know where Viktoria keeps the lightbulbs!" I heard the door open. "Viktoria! Where is a lightbulb? I need one for my office; it's going out!"

"Brandon, you just changed it," I said not looking up from the magazine I had lying in my lap. "It will not go out; just switch the light on and off. That should work."

"All right, I'll try that." I heard the door close.

"Okay, girls," I whispered. "Now!"

"Oh my God! Who are you? What are you doing here? How did you get in my office? Are you Melisa's friends? She's not here. Viktoria! Get downstairs right now! Two of Melisa's friends are here! What are they doing in my office?"

"Brandon, calm down. These girls are the ones you said were only spirits. There is nothing we can do for them, remember? They heard what you said, and they are here to reason with you and explain."

He looked at me. "I know you put them up to this."

"You see, Brandon, you are sensitive to them. Do you feel them? Do you see them? They want to tell you why they are here. They want to know what I can do for them, so that they can cross over."

"How long have they been here? Are they with us all the time?"

"Yes, most of the time. Azalea just came in; she was watching over your mother. Gabriellele, the tall one, she is with us. She likes to talk to Lacey."

"What are you saying? She likes to talk to Lacey? Why are you getting Lacey into this mess?"

"Lacey is very sensitive; she sees Gabriellele and others. She is the one who told me that there was a lady next to me the day I came home from the hospital. She has been talking to my mom and Babushka."

"Since … when has she had this psychic ability?"

"I don't know when, but she recently told me she has been talking to the dead."

"I can't win, can I? If it's not my wife, it's my daughter! Go ahead! Do what you need to do, but I know there will be things you might see you will not like. I can feel it."

"What do you mean, Brandon? Is there something you know that I don't?"

He shook his head. "I'm just overreacting; I don't know anything. You've had your fun. I need to go back to my files."

I left.

\* \* \*

Brandon turned around and saw the man in the corner of the room. "Samuel, we need to talk. Viktoria is going to find out sooner or later about it. I need your help; this thing is getting deeper and deeper. If she finds out, she will never forgive me."

"Brandon, we still have time. She has to find the twins first, and even then, she will not know about them. So there is nothing you should worry about."

"I wish I never got involved with you people."

"Well, it's too late. You wanted to be successful and have power. You should have thought about that before you agreed to this. You knew what you were getting into."

"What about these two spirits in my house? What are we going to do? Would they say anything about me to Viktoria? Then what?"

"You don't need to worry. They're both forbidden to talk; they won't say much anyway. They're trying to help Viktoria and trying to stop us from killing the rest. We need to get rid of all of them; we don't need them anymore. They are of no use to us. Two of them were touched by Leila, but we do not know who they are because they were all born at the same time. Why do you care anyway? Your twins are already dead. They all have to die; we cannot let any of them live."

"God, what have you done? Samuel, do not touch my family! Keep your demons away from them! I do not want you to bother them. Do we understand each other?"

"I cannot promise you that, not until all the demon-born babies vanish from the face of the earth. I have stopped your mom from talking about the twins. If I hadn't, your psychic wife would have known everything by now."

"I cannot believe you! You hurt my mother after all I have done for you! I am telling you, keep away from my family! I am warning you!"

"Brandon," Viktoria asked through the door, "who are you talking to at this time of night? It's getting late. I am going to sleep, you should too. We have an early morning."

"Okay, honey. I'll be up soon. I'm talking to someone at work. One of my patients is acting up again. Go to sleep; I will be up as soon as I am done."

\* \* \*

"I cannot think of anything now, Gabriellele," I said to her as I sat at the kitchen table. "Now I know there is something that Brandon is involved in that he does not want me to know about. I am absolutely sure of that. Whatever it is, I've got to get to the bottom of it."

"Viktoria, who is Samuel? Brandon was talking to him after we left his office."

"I don't know, but Brandon said he was talking to someone from work." After a yawn, I said, "Okay girls, I need to sleep, so I'll see you both tomorrow. We're going to see Nelly."

I lay in bed, waiting for sleep to capture me. Just as it almost took over, Brandon walked in. He looked worried and concerned. He kept mumbling, "What have I done?" I pretended to be asleep; I did not want to question him. I knew he would only get more upset.

But all night, I kept wondering who Samuel was. I knew all his coworkers, but I'd never heard of Samuel before.

I got up early to get the kids ready for school. When Brandon showed up—not looking much better than he did last night—I asked him to drop them at school. I wanted to get to the hospital and see how Nelly was doing.

When I arrived at the hospital, I saw Doctor Justin getting out of his car, so I rushed over to see him and ask him if Brandon had ever brought up Samuel to him.

"Good morning, Doctor Justin. You're here early this morning."

"I came in to see Nelly, and then I have some operations. I might not have time to see her afterward, so I thought I would see her before."

"That is nice of you."

"Nelly is someone special to me; I will do whatever it takes." He looked behind me. "Where is Brandon? He's upstairs already?"

"Oh no, Brandon's dropping the kids off at school and then he is going to work. Samuel called late last night; he said there was a problem with one of his patients."

"That's strange. My wife was on duty. I don't think I've ever heard of Samuel before. Are you sure you didn't get the name wrong?"

"No, I don't think so. That's what Brandon told me."

"It must be someone new then. Linda never mentioned any problems at the hospital last night. She usually calls and tells me about them the next day."

I decided to change the topic. "Anyway, what do you think about Nelly? Will her speech get better?"

"In a couple of days. Some speech therapy sessions would help her talk better. But be easy on her; she needs lots of rest, and less anxiety would help. Otherwise, I'm sure she will do fine. Nelly is a strong person."

"The night when she had the heart attack, Nelly wanted to tell me something. She said it was important; she was excited and trembling. I had never seen her like that before. I told her whatever it was, it could wait until she was feeling better. Now when I see Nelly, I feel bad because of it."

"Then let's go in together; she might not say anything yet. In addition, I will tell her not to get herself tired by moving or talking too much."

"Thank you, Doctor Justin. 1 know it's an excellent idea if it comes from you."

We arrived at her room about ten minutes later. "Good morning, Nelly," I said. Doctor Justin was following me. "How are we doing this morning? Look, Doctor Justin is here to see you too."

"I feel much better this morning. Melisa and I had some juice, and she left for school a few minutes ago."

"Let me see the chart to make sure you did get better," the doctor said before picking up her chart at the end of her bed. "By the looks of it, you're right. Much better. Keep it up, Nelly! You will be out of here tomorrow morning."

I grabbed her arm. "Nelly, tomorrow, you can come home! That's wonderful news!"

"I will let you go home as long as you promise me that you will relax and have no excitement around you—and less chatting."

"We promise, and I will swear to it, Doctor Justin. Right, Nelly?"

She sighed. I could tell she wasn't happy, but she was going to do it. "If you say so."

"Nelly," Doctor Justin said looking at her. "I want you to promise me, or I will not let you go home."

"Justin, I hope you know what you're doing. Bargaining on this … you know it's impossible to do that."

"Well, Nelly. What do think? Is it a promise?"

"Good morning, everyone! How are you doing this morning, Nelly?"

"I am doing just fine, Doctor Damien, but these two are not."

"What, Nelly?"

"They're both trying to bargain with me before Doctor Justin lets me out tomorrow."

Doctor Damien laughed. "Well, can I be a witness to that, Doctor Justin?"

"It will be my great honor."

"You are in on this too, Damien," Nelly said with a hint of betrayal in her voice.

"You can say that we just want you to get better as soon as possible. I heard you make the best brownies."

"Now I understand," she said with a knowing smile, "why everyone is so concerned about me." She sighed. "Okay, then that is the deal."

"Nelly, the kids are so happy that you are going to stay with us. They fixed up the bedroom downstairs for you. Cameron and I will pick you up, and then you have the rest of the day to do what he has planned for you. Nelly, do you need anything? At home, I mean. Do you need me to pick up something?"

"Yes, dear, but we will get it on the way to your house. Viktoria, I still have something to tell you; it is very important that I do this soon."

"Nelly, I told you before; when you feel better, I am all ears for you, and Brandon wants to know as well."

"You told him?"

"I am so sorry. I didn't know that he wasn't supposed to know. The day you got sick, Brandon asked me what made you so upset—what caused you to have the heart attack. I told him you wanted to talk to me about something you had overheard."

"Maybe it is for the best if he is there when I tell you. I want everything to come out at the same time."

"All right then. When the time comes, we will think about that. But for now, I want you to get some rest. I'm going to go downstairs and get something to drink, okay, Nelly?"

When she nodded, I patted her hand and walked out of the room. As I was walking down the hallway, my phone rang. "Hello?"

"Hi, Mom," Lacey said. "How is Grandma Nelly doing?"

"She's fine, Lacey. Why are you calling me? Is everything okay at school? You're not sick, are you?"

"Mom, can you come to my school? I need you to see someone."

I walked back to the room and opened the door. Nelly looked over at me. "Nelly, I have to go to Lacey's school. She needs me there, but I won't be long."

"Go, dear, don't make her wait. She needs you. I hope she's not sick or anything."

"She said she's fine, but she wants to show me something. She has a project that she needs help with. Nelly, if Greg comes by, do not tell him I went to the school; he will panic."

"Don't worry. I will tell him you have gone to pick up something from my house."

"Thanks, Nelly. I love you."

# Chapter 8

## *Saving Mrs. Adams*

"Mom," Lacey said when I got back on the phone with her, "I'm concerned about one of my teachers. She recently started teaching in our school. I think some sort of entity is following her around; it is a dark shadow. I don't know what to do."

"Lacey, don't do anything. Stay away from the dark shadow; do you understand me? Do not get any closer or have contact with it. Do not let it know you can see it. I'm coming over there now. One thing you can do is find out when your teacher's birthday is. That's very important."

"Okay, I'll find out and call you."

"Okay, baby, I'm calling Michael and Greg to meet me over there. This could be very dangerous; stay away from your teacher! Tell her I need to talk to her; it's important."

I hung up with Lacey and called Michael. "Michael, I'm going over to Lacey's school. She said that she has seen an entity around her new teacher; she said it is a black shadow. Can you call Greg and come over there? I need help from both of you."

"Yeah, sure. Don't go inside without me, okay? We both will go and ask for the teacher."

"Okay, Michael. I'll wait right in front of the school for you; we'll get Lacey too. I don't want her to hang around there any longer."

I hung up with Michael and closed my eyes. "Okay, Babushka. It's time to use those jinns; I need their presence at Lacey's high school. She needs protection."

"Okay, Viktoria," I heard Babushka say. "Shia and Zanah are on the way. They will appear as humans, so you do not have to worry about what they look like. They will talk to you telepathically, so when you get there, they will tell you exactly where they are."

"Babushka, please tell them to stay with Lacey. She may be in danger! They have to tell her that I sent them, so she should not be scared of them. Maybe I should just call her now."

"Hi, Lacey," I said when she picked up her phone.

"Yes, Mom?"

"Lacey, Babushka has sent two jinn to stay with you and protect you. They will communicate with you through telepathy so listen carefully. Don't worry; they are there for your protection. I am on my way; I'm two blocks away from the school, so wait for me patiently."

"Mom, Greg just got here. I'm with him in the office."

"Lacey, that's impossible! That can't be Greg; he would never come to your school without my permission. Stay away from him!"

"There were two kids who brought me to the office, but they didn't talk. I think I understood what they were saying by looking into their eyes. They're here next to me; they will not leave."

"Lacey, if you understand them, what are they saying to you? Tell me!"

"They are telling me to stay with them and not to talk to Greg."

"Listen to them, Lacey. I am by the school door; I see Michael is here as well. Do not say anything. We are coming in." I hung up and walked over to Michael. "Greg is inside. He asked to see Lacey."

"That's impossible, Viktoria. I just spoke to Greg; he said he has to stop and get gas. That will take him another five minutes."

"Okay then, let's go inside and see. That's what I told Lacey—that it can't be Greg, I mean. I told her to stay away from him."

"Mom!" Lacey said as she ran up to me. "I am so glad to see you!"

"Where is Greg, Lacey?"

"I have not seen him. He just went outside. He said he left something in his car." She turned around and looked at the two people sitting on the chairs. "And these two are the friends I told you about, Mom."

I silently thanked them, and they looked at me saying that it was nothing and they would stick around there until I told them to leave. I was glad they were there; I never knew that the jinn could be so obedient to their masters.

"Michael, talk to the principal and tell her we need to talk to Mrs. Adams. Ask if they can call her down."

"Mom," Lacey said, "Mrs. Adams is in the teacher's room; she knows you are coming."

"Lacey, where are your friends?"

"They are next to Mrs. Adams. I told them to watch over her."

I gave her a pat on the shoulder and smiled. "That's my girl!"

We walked to the teacher's lounge, and Lacey pointed out her teacher. "There she is." She took a breath before knocking on the door. "Mrs. Adams, we're here!"

"Hi, Mrs. Adams. I am Viktoria, and this is my partner, Michael. We need to ask you a few questions, if that's okay with you."

"I know who you are and why you are here," Mrs. Adams said. "And yes, we need to talk."

"Mrs. Adams, do you think you can leave? We need to talk somewhere else."

"Um, sure. I have no classes for the rest of the day; we can leave now."

"Where would you like to go, Mrs. Adams?" Michael asked.

"Anywhere but my place."

"All right," I said. "Then let's go to the station."

Right before we left, I said, "Michael, let me go back inside and tell Lacey we're leaving so she can go back to class with her friends."

He nodded and continued leading Mrs. Adams out as I walked over to Lacey. "We're leaving. Go back to your class. These two will be watching over you, so I don't want you to worry. Oh, by the way, their names are Shia and Zanah."

"Yes, I know that, Mom. They told me already. I have to go to swimming class now."

"Call me when you get home. Also, don't mention what happened today to your father, okay?"

"Right, Mom. I won't say anything. I love you."

I told her I loved her too before I walked out the door.

Michael came up to me. "Greg just made it. We're going to the station. Meet us over there."

Greg came up to us. "Guys, you won't believe what happened! I thought I didn't have any gas, so I stopped to get some. But then the pump wouldn't let the gas go in the tank! When I asked the guy why this was happening, he asked if he could look. I let him, so he went into the car and started it. Then he said, 'You have a full tank of gas.'"

"We do believe you. Wait until you hear what we have to tell you."

"What is it, Viktoria?"

"Not so fast, Greg. You have to wait until we get to the station."

"You're going to kill me with suspense!"

"Maybe later, but now we need you. We need to go now, Greg, and Michael will follow us."

I thought of something. "Michael, we shouldn't go to the station; we should to go to the chapel with Mrs. Adams and Greg!"

"You're right, Viktoria. Let me call Father Wilson; he might be able to help us."

"I am sorry to cut into the conversation," Mrs. Adams said. "But I am Muslim."

"Oh!" I said. "I'm so sorry. We didn't think of that, because of your last name."

"That's all right," she said with a slight smile. "I am married to an Englishman who has converted to Islam but kept his family name."

"That's good news, Mrs. Adams. How do you know everything about us and the other stuff we have to do?"

"Angel Leila told me she would appear in my dreams, and recently, she told me that I would be saved, that my nightmares would be ended by three people. She said they would find me, and not to seek them."

"I cannot believe this, Viktoria!" said Greg. "If Leila knows all of this, why can't she stop Lilith?"

"I know," said Mrs. Adams. "We should go to a mosque. We always go to one; I'll call my husband to meet us there."

"You call him," I said. "I'll get you another imam; his name is Muhammad. He is well known and does the exorcisms."

"Where is this mosque, Mrs. Adams?"

"It's ten blocks away. My husband will meet us over there."

"Greg, I need to call Lacey and have her send her two friends over here. We need them to check the place out before we go in."

I took out my cell phone and dialed her number. When she picked up, I said, "Lacey, are your friends with you?"

"No, Mom. They said you needed help and left."

"What do you mean?"

"Mrs. Adams is still here. She said she is waiting for you, Mom."

"Okay, Lacey. Stay next to Mrs. Adams. Tell her to go to the nearest church or mosque and stay with her! Also ask her husband to meet her there too."

"All right, Mom. What's going on? I'm scared. I thought she already left with you to go to the station. When I told her so, she said she never saw you or Michael."

"Just do what I tell you."

"Viktoria, look! There's an accident. Someone's hurt; let's see if they need our help."

"Michael, stay where you are! Don't move! Look, there are two policemen coming up to my car."

"Ma'am, this road is closed. You're going to have to make a detour. Please make a U-turn."

"Michael, the road is closed. We have to make a detour. Tell Mrs. Adams that we have to turn back and go a different way."

"Okay, Viktoria, she said there is another shortcut we can take. Follow us, all right?"

"Greg, call Michael and tell him to stop the car in a few hundred feet. Tell him your car is making a noise, and we need to go with him."

"Get your stuff ready. We need to vanquish a demon or jinn."

"What happened, Viktoria?"

"Just spoke to Lacey, and she said Mrs. Adams is still at school waiting for us. Gabriellele confirmed that this is a setup. We need to do this fast before they hurt the real Mrs. Adams and us. Greg, do it right now!"

"Viktoria, when we stop, get the holy water ready. Throw it on her and don't forget to say, 'Came from hell and you shall stay in hell! You are forbidden here!' Don't forget."

"All right, Greg, let's do it now."

"I'm calling Michael and telling him to stop the car."

"Go ahead."

"Michael, you need to stop the car. We have to come with you," Greg said into his phone.

"What happened?"

"My car started to make a weird noise; we need a ride."

"Okay, I'll come get you."

"Viktoria and Greg!" we heard someone say. "Stop whatever you are about to do! She is the real Mrs. Adams! Do not do it!"

"Babushka, is that you?"

"Yes and that is Mrs. Adams; she has an allergy to holy water. She will die as soon as you throw it."

"But, Babushka, Gabriellele and Lacey, and those two jinns … this doesn't make any sense."

"Viktoria, those two people were real police officers, and they spoke to you. The ones I have given to you were next to Lacey. Besides, Lacey was swimming! She would not be able to pick up her phone! It is the demon!"

"Greg, did you heard that?"

"Yes, Viktoria. Just leave it and listen to your father."

"Honey," my father said softly, "listen to me. Take her to a mosque before it is too late."

"Okay, Babushka."

When we got to Michael's car, I asked, "Mrs. Adams, are you okay?"

"Yes, I am now. I heard what was going on. I do not blame you for suspecting something different. I am sorry that this has happened."

"No, Mrs. Adams, we are sorry. Let's get you to the mosque as soon as possible."

"My name is Alia. I would be happier if you called me by my first name."

"All right then, Alia. Why didn't you say anything to try to stop us?"

"Your dad has been watching over me for a long time, and he said he would talk to you. He said that he was sent by Leila to watch over me and to teach me how to use my powers wisely."

"What powers? How does my dad know about this? He never said anything to me."

"I am one of the twins who was touched by Leila. I have recently come to the United States. My husband's job transferred him here. He is a scientist as well as an imam."

"Why did he transfer here?"

"They were doing research on human cells, and he thought it would be better for me to be back where I was born."

"Where were you born?"

"I was born on Long Island in New York, like Damien and the rest of the demon girls. I am one of the twins born that night, but my adopted parents never mentioned anything about the other. We moved to England when I was a toddler, and since then, they have tried to keep me safe. But I know it is time for me to fight for what I believe. I know that I am not a demon child; my biological father was a Lucifer worshipper. I believe in God, even though they have been telling me otherwise."

"What happened to your biological parents? Are they still alive?"

"I think so."

"Do you know where they live?"

"No, not yet. I've been told that my biological parents were told that their twins died at birth. Even when I found out, my adopted parents would never tell me who I am. They said that it would hurt them more."

"Which hospital were you born in?"

"I believe it was Long Island General Hospital."

I couldn't believe my ears. "Which hospital did you say?"

"Long Island General."

"When?"

"February 14, 1982."

"That's impossible! If I remember right, I am the only one who had twins in that hospital that night. However, I had two boys." I shook my head. "There must be a mistake; it can't be!" It couldn't be. I was the only one to have twins at the hospital that night. It made no sense; I was so confused.

"Maybe you're right, but my parents told me the night of our birth, all the boys were stillborn, except my twin who was touched by Leila at birth. She saved him and gave him to another family who had lost their boy. They switched the babies and gave me to another family who lost their boy as well that night."

"We are here," Michael said.

"There is my husband out front, waiting for us," Alia said. She turned to me. "Viktoria, I do not need to be baptized or have an exorcism because of Leila. I have been protected from the demons; they cannot kill me. The reason I have brought you here is we need to talk where no demon entity can hear us."

"Okay, then, let's go inside and talk about it."

We went inside and found a place to sit. Once we were settled, she said, "As I told you, I have a twin sibling who is male. We have to find him. Last time I searched for him, it said in the records that he had died, which is impossible. We have both been protected by Leila from Lilith's jinns and demons. Only the Angel of Death can take our souls when he is ordered by the Lord. I have been told that you, I, and others will be able to find him."

"How are we going to do that?"

"We need to astral travel, and Leila will show us his image. This is the only way."

"Will Leila tell us where he is? That's impossible because Lilith is after Leila. Any chance she gets, Lilith will try to destroy her, and this will start the angels' war."

"Leila does not want that."

"When can we do this?"

"In two weeks, I will let you know, but I have to follow my instructions. Make sure everyone goes to bed at the same time and concentrate on meeting us in the mosque; that is the only way. Now that you are here, look around and get a feeling for it, so you know how and where to meet us. One thing, when we all do this, our bodies have to be watched over by loved ones who can protect us from demons; they will try to take over our bodies. For instance, your mom can go into your body until you've returned."

"Greg, you can have your uncle take over your body, meanwhile," I said.

"Don't do any readings or demon hunting until then. We need your full concentration."

"What about Brandon? He will know something is up."

"I am sorry, Viktoria. You're not allowed to tell him anything at all. Make sure you have the kids sleeping together in one room; Shia and Zanah will protect them. Take Melisa's room for you to sleep in."

"I can take Lacey's room; I don't think Melisa will leave her room."

"Lacey's room is too active; they know she is sensitive. They're always there, and they know she has powers as well. It's okay for them to sleep in her room but not you."

"Gabriellele and Azalea will join us too."

"What about Carmella? Will she join us?"

"No, Carmella can't join us because she has been given a second chance by Leila. She was awarded a new body, and now she is taking care of her baby."

"I am so happy to hear that! I was worried about her; I thought demons might find her and hurt her and the baby."

"So I am hoping to see everyone here in two weeks. Don't forget, Viktoria, don't say anything to Brandon, not a word."

"How do you know Brandon, Alia?"

"When Brandon comes, you will know the truth. Until then, don't tell him or mention anything about me."

"I won't." I looked at my watch. "It's getting late. I have to go back to the hospital to see Grandma Nelly. We'll talk later."

"Viktoria, don't worry about Nelly; she will be just fine. She has been watched over."

"I trust you with all of my heart, Alia."

When Alia lifted up her arm, I saw a sort of a handprint under her arm. It was lighter than her skin; I knew I'd seen the same birthmark somewhere before.

"Alia, what is that under your arm?"

"It is a birthmark I was given by Leila. She was the first one to hold us up when we were born, and my twin will have the same birthmark on his right arm."

"That is good to know; I am glad you mentioned that."

"All right then," Michael said. "I am leaving as well. Viktoria, wait. We're coming with you to see Nelly."

"What a day it was. Greg, I cannot believe we fell for that! I am so glad we were warned."

"You know, Viktoria; we have to be more cautious next time."

"We have to thank God. We have also found one of the angels. Now how are we going to find the other sibling?"

"We have to do what she told us to do and wait until you hear from her," Greg said. He put his hands into his pockets. "Viktoria, something has been bothering me."

"If it is about Brandon, it bothers me too, but you heard Alia. Don't mention anything to him."

"I don't understand how he is involved with this. I bet this is what Nelly wanted to talk to you about."

"He had better have a damn good explanation when we're finished with the case."

"Viktoria, didn't he warn you that you should not to get involved in this case and that people would get hurt?"

"Yes, he did."

"Why? He could've been more open."

"Greg, I'm sure he has his own reasons. Also he needs to protect his family."

"That's not enough for me. He knows what I do, and this will eventually come out."

"Viktoria, you are too hard on him; give him a chance to explain first. Try not to jump to any conclusions."

"Okay. Let's go upstairs and make sure everything is okay with Nelly. She will be very happy to see you, Greg."

We went into her hospital room. "We're back, Nelly! How are you doing? I'm sorry I had to leave you, but I was in a rush."

"That's okay, baby. I wasn't alone. Melisa stopped by after school along with that young doctor. Can't remember his name right now, but he said if I wanted to go home today, I could. What do you say, Viktoria? Do you think I can?"

"Of course, Nelly. Let's get you ready, and then we will surprise everyone when we get home."

"That's a marvelous idea, Viktoria dear. Can we stop by the store for some ice cream? I know Cameron would love that."

"Whatever your heart desires, Nelly; just ask."

*   *   *

"Everything is set," I said a little while later, after I got all the forms filled out. "Let's go home!"

"Greg," Nelly asked as she walked to the bathroom so that she could get changed into her normal clothes, "did you see that young doctor?"

"Which one?"

"I think she means Damien," I guessed.

"No, but I did see Doctor Justin. He said he would be here in few minutes to see Nelly off."

"It's so nice of him to do that. I just remembered, Viktoria, Melisa went with Doctor Damien to have something to eat."

"That's okay, Nelly. I'll call Melisa to come home when she is done."

"Hi, Doctor Justin, we have been waiting for you. We decided to take Nelly home tonight. I believe Doctor Damien has told her we can."

"Yes, I know. I told him to tell Nelly, so she must be happy." He gave her a smile as she came out of the bathroom. "Brandon isn't here?"

"Oh. No, he's not, and he doesn't know his mom is coming home today. Matter of fact, no one knows; it's a surprise!"

"Okay," he said with a smile. "Don't let me keep you any longer, Nelly. I will come over to see you soon. Viktoria, let's not meet under bad circumstances anymore. Last time, it was when you had the twins, if you remember."

"Yes, I do. You were here that night when I had the boys. That was a crazy night."

"Yes, you're absolutely right; it was a crazy night. Remember the lights went out and our system was out. As I remember, a few boys were stillborns."

"I do remember very well, because one of my boys was stillborn. The next day, my other boy died."

"Your other baby—as I remember—Viktoria, was not a boy. We only had one set of twins born that night, and that was your twins. They were not twin boys; it was a boy and a girl!"

"You are mistaken, Justin. I had twin boys. As I held the second boy, the light went out, and you went to see what was going on."

"Yes, I did, but I'm absolutely sure it was not two boys and that you did not have a stillborn, because when I came back, I put the hats on the babies—a pink hat on the girl and a blue one on the boy. Brandon was next to me."

"Then where are my babies, Justin?" I all but screamed.

"I don't know, Viktoria. Every time I asked about the twins, Brandon never said anything about them. He said nothing about the twins being dead."

"You are wrong!" I shouted. I couldn't hold it back any longer. Talking about that night was hard enough, but now he was telling me that my babies were not dead! They were, in fact, possibly very much alive! "You are confused! It was a hell of an active night, and you could have easily made a mistake! I have an idea; when I come over, we will ask Brandon about this."

"You know what? I'll check the files from when the systems were down. We always put the files into the system. I know I'm right!"

"Just remember, Justin, don't mentioned anything to Brandon. He has taken it hard and still is not over the twins. Maybe this is the reason he did not say anything to you."

"All right, I will call you when I find out anything. I'll see you all in a couple of days."

# Chapter 9

## *Grandma Nelly Comes Home*

"Did you hear that, Nelly? I think Justin has been working way too hard lately. Or he is going senile. I don't understand how he can tell me that my twins are not dead. And on top of that, he is telling me that I did not have a stillborn! What the hell is wrong with him? He was probably drunk that night, or something!"

"I don't know what to tell you, Viktoria."

"Nelly, wasn't that night—the night I went to the hospital for the twins—wasn't that the night his daughter went missing?"

"Yes, it was that night. But his daughter is not missing."

"They found out what happened to her?"

"You don't know? They found his daughter that night."

"How …" I asked in shock. I had never heard this story. "Where was she?"

"She was with me."

"What do you mean?"

"Well, it was a long time ago, and they needed a babysitter. His wife had an emergency and had to go somewhere, so she called me and asked if she could leave Emily—that's the daughter's name—with me. She forgot to tell her husband, since she was in a big rush. When he came home and did not find them, he called the police officers."

"Then how did they find out Emily was with you?"

"The officers went to the babysitter's house, but she was not there. The babysitter's sister told them she had taken her husband to the hospital because he had appendicitis. It was the same hospital Justin was in."

"Then what happened?"

"Well, the officer told Justin the sitter was there and asked the wife where Emily was. Of course, she told them that Emily was with me. Then Justin called me to confirm that she was telling the truth and I said yes."

"Poor Justin. I know why he does not remember much of that night. I didn't know about this. The night of the birth of the twins, they called him downstairs for an emergency. When he came back, he looked so worried. When I asked him what was wrong, he said his daughter was missing." I sighed as I drove on. "Well, we're almost home. The kids will be so happy to see you."

"Dear, do not forget the ice cream."

"Yes, we have to celebrate your homecoming! We better get extra or else Cameron will make me go back for more. Remind me to call Melisa and tell her to come home."

We stopped at a store to get what we needed. When we got back into the car, I said, "We got everything we need, Nelly. We can hit the road now. I cannot wait to see the look on their faces when they see you!"

"Don't forget to call Melisa."

"Oh! Good thing you reminded me!" I took out my phone and dialed her number. "Hi, Melisa, where are you?"

"I am with Doctor Damien; we're going to see Grandma Nelly."

"Honey, Grandma Nelly is with me. I'm taking her home. Why don't you come home? If you like, Damien can join us in celebrating Grandma's homecoming."

"I'll ask him, Mom."

"All right then. We're almost home, so don't spoil this. It's a surprise."

"Okay, Mom. I won't." And then she hung up.

We got out of the car, and I grabbed all the stuff before going to the front door where Nelly was already waiting. "We're home."

"Isn't that strange? The lights are off. Shouldn't they be home?"

"Yes, Lacey and Cameron should be home by now. Maybe they have both fallen asleep. We will find out when we get inside." I opened the door and turned on the light in the hallway. "Hi, guys. I have someone with me!"

"Surprise!" Lacey, Cameron, and Melisa yelled. I looked around and saw signs that Cameron must have made—they were messily written—that said, "Welcome home!"

"Oh my goodness!" Nelly said in shock. "What a wonderful surprise!"

"How did you all know about Nelly coming home?"

"Well, Mom," Melisa said, "when you called, we were getting ready."

"How did you find out?"

"Damien called the hospital to check on Grandma Nelly. The nurse told him that she had been discharged from the hospital."

"We came straight home to surprise you guys," I said. I looked at Melisa. "When I called, you were at home already." It was a statement, not a question.

"You got it, Mom," she answered with a smile.

"How about an ice cream cake, Mom?" Cameron asked.

"Yes, how about it?" I handed the bag with the slowly melting cake to Melisa, who gave me a look I couldn't understand. "What?"

"Well, it's just that Dad already got an ice cream cake."

That was when I looked at who was sitting on the couch. "Brandon, you're here! I didn't expect you!"

"Yes, well, when the kids told me about Mom coming home, I had to leave everything and come. I ran to the store to get Mom's favorite ice cream cake."

"Nelly, you never mentioned a favorite ice cream cake."

"Mom," Cameron said, "Grandma's favorite is double-chocolate ice cream fudge cake."

"Well, yes, and I know you did ask me, Viktoria, but I couldn't remember what I liked." She turned to the rest of the family. "It is so nice of you to do this. Thank you so very much; you have overdone it!"

"We love you, Grandma Nelly!" Cameron said before running over to her and giving her a hug.

"And a special thanks to Cameron, who remembered my favorite cake."

"It was my pleasure to remember, Grandma Nelly," he said with a grin.

After we had some cake, I said, "Everyone, it's time to let Grandma Nelly go get some rest; it has been a long day for her, so let's get her to her room. Lacey and Cameron, it's time to finish your homework and then off to bed." I turned to Nelly.

"Brandon will help you get settled in your room, and as soon as I clear the kitchen, I will join you."

"Come on, Mom," Brandon said as he took his mother's arm. "Let's get you to your room."

"Thank you, Brandon. I just do not want to be a burden on you."

"Nelly, what are you saying?" I said with a shake of my head. "I am going to disregard that."

"Mom, you know that you are always welcome here."

"It's nice to hear that," she said before going off with Brandon.

I felt a presence in the house. "Gabriellele, is that you?"

"Yes, Viktoria. I'm in Lacey's room."

"Can you go to Nelly's room and find out what is going on in there?"

"What do you mean?"

"I do not want Brandon to force Nelly to tell him what she was going to tell me."

"All right, but …"

"You have something to tell me?"

"Yes. You know he can see me and feel it too."

"You're right; I forgot about that." I thought for a moment. "Gabriellele, go and whisper in his ear that I need him."

"I can do that. I am in Lacey's room if you need me. I'm helping her with her social studies homework."

"Where is Azalea?"

"She is also with Lacey, helping her with biology homework."

"Whoa, Lacey has got it made. That would explain why she has been getting great marks lately. I did not know you could do that. I need to talk to her."

"It's nothing, Viktoria; when she needs help, she asks us a question and we assist her."

"All right then. But then make sure she does not abuse it. And, Gabriellele, don't forget to tell Lacey."

I couldn't get over what Justin had said earlier. I wondered if he was right about that. No, that would be impossible; I had seen the second boy when he was in an incubator, but I never saw the stillborn. Why didn't they let me hold him? I had requested to do so.

"Viktoria," Brandon said as he came into the room, "I got your message; it was not funny. ... Viktoria? Did you hear what I said? Viktoria?"

I was lost so deeply in thought, I didn't hear him. So when he touched me on my shoulder, I jumped. "Oh, God, Brandon! You scared the hell out of me!"

"What is wrong with you? You look like you've seen a ghost. Not that you don't on a regular basis. You even send your messages through them," he ended with a smirk.

"Ha, ha!" I give a sarcastic laugh. "If that was supposed to be a joke, you missed it by a mile."

"Whatever. Why did you call?"

"I simply wanted to talk to you. How was your day? You've seemed a bit down recently. Is everything okay?"

"It's the new hospital; I do not know if it will finish on time. I have been suggested for a new position as head of the hospital over in Virginia, and I am seriously thinking of taking it."

"Hold on. You are going way too fast. Why have you never mentioned this before? What do you mean, you are thinking about taking the position? Were you not going to tell us? Were you going to come home one day and just go, 'Surprise, honey! We are moving to Virginia!'"

"I thought you would be happy about it. You've always hoped to move from here, haven't you? This is our chance!"

"That was several years back, Brandon! Now Melisa is ready to start her internship, and Lacey has another year in high school before she graduates."

"Well, don't be too concerned about Melisa. I will transfer her internship to my medical center, and Lacey would do much better in the schools over there."

"What about my job? And your mom?"

"We will take her with us. And you can get another job over there, or you can start your own business. And can I just say that I do not like the idea of Melisa seeing Damien? I don't want her to rush into anything."

"Brandon, don't change the topic. Besides, they're only friends; he is giving her advice on her internship. What's wrong with that? But what about the job?"

"As I said, I'm thinking about it."

"I know you, Brandon; tell me the truth. Have you accepted the job? Don't lie to me."

He looked away for a moment before looking back at me. "Yes, I have taken the position. It was the best offer ever, so I took it! What are you going to do about it?"

"Don't yell. Your mom can hear us."

"Whatever. I have done this for the family."

"We will talk about this later. I do not want Nelly or the children to be upset. Do you understand me?"

"I am going out for a little walk," Brandon said before walking out the door.

"I hope Nelly didn't hear us fighting," I mumbled.

"Viktoria," Azalea said, "do you want me to go check on her?"

"That's a good idea."

A few seconds later, she came back. "She's sleeping. I am sure she did not hear you at all."

"Thanks. I hope the kids didn't hear us either."

"No, Viktoria, they're all in their beds sleeping. I checked on them as well."

"Gabriellele, I'm going to go upstairs. I will be doing an astral travel. I have to see where Brandon has gone to. Azalea can stay with Nelly. I will call my mom to watch over my body."

"Viktoria, don't you think you are overreacting?"

"No, Azalea, I don't think so. I would appreciate it if you stayed next to Nelly. Gabriellele, you can watch the kids. Don't worry; I'm taking Shia and Zanah with me." I went up to my room and sat on my bed. "Mom, I need you! Where are you? ... Come on, Mom! I know you're around here! Please, please, Mom."

"Yes, Viktoria, I am here now."

"Where were you?"

"I had another thing to do."

"Well, I need your help."

"What is it? You are fuming. What happened?"

"It's a long story; I'll tell you later, but you have to do what I ask you to do, Mom."

"Don't keep me in suspense. Tell me."

"Mom, please take over my body in case Nelly or the kids get up. I seriously need to do this."

"Do not tell me you are going to have an out-of-body experience? It's too dangerous, especially now!"

"Yes, Mom, I have to find out what is going on with Brandon."

She sighed. "Okay, baby. However, your father, does he know what you are about to do you? You should consult your father before you go. You should talk to him first."

"No. Dad already sent two of his helpers; I am taking them with me, so don't worry; I will be just fine."

"Viktoria, I still think that doing this out-of-body ritual is dangerous."

"Mom, please listen to what I am telling you. You just take over my body until I come back. If you don't want to do it, fine. I'm still doing it."

"Baby, you know better than that; I cannot do it."

"Yes, you can."

"I don't know what to tell you." She fell silent for a moment, and then she took a breath and said, "Go ahead; I will take over. But if you sense any kind of danger, you have to come back. Please don't chase any demons either! They will drag you to the hole!"

"Okay, I promise. Mom, can you grab his key on the table for me? I might be able to feel where he is."

I started to focus deeply. Finally, I was almost there. I was able to see Shia and Zanah. It was helping me to go to deeper and deeper. I thought they knew where Brandon was; they wanted me to hold on to them. Yes, I made it. I couldn't believe I was actually doing this! Spying on my husband! But there was nothing else I could do. He had become a different man—more … aggressive.

*My God, he is two houses away from Alia's house. What the hell is he doing? How does he know her?* I couldn't believe what I was seeing. "Shia, get closer; I want to see what is going on." He was looking over a picture of a girl who was not Melisa or Lacey. Who was it?

Oh no! Alia and her husband were coming back from somewhere! I hoped they would not notice his car. Thank the Lord! They drove right by and did not see him!

"Shia, let's go see what is going on."

"Viktoria, don't go close to the house."

"Who is that?"

"It's me, Babushka."

"What are you doing, Babushka?"

"Watching over Alia."

"Then you know that Brandon is here."

"Yes, I do. Alia knows he is here too."

I was so confused. This case was like *The Da Vinci Code*; it was all puzzles.

"Don't worry, Viktoria; you will solve the puzzle soon."

"But, Babushka, why does it seem like Brandon is involved in this case?"

"Alia has been diligent in not informing Brandon on this matter."

"Look over there, Babushka. Who is that person right next to Brandon's car? I am going closer to see what's going on."

"Viktoria, don't. Go back home, and call Brandon right away and ask him to come home."

"Why, Babushka?"

"That man is a demon."

"Why would a demon follow Brandon?"

"Listen, instead of answering that question, I am going to say that you should just go back and do what I am asking you to do. Alia could be in danger."

# Chapter 10

## *Lilin*

When I tried to return to my body, I got the shock of my life.

I could not see it.

I knew Mom had taken over my body, but I needed it and thought she was downstairs as me.

Fortunately, I was wrong. Mom was in Lacey's room telling her that my body was being taken over by another soul.

I went downstairs. There was my body walking around and checking the house with great care. Now she—I—was going into Nelly's room.

I went into Lacey's room. At least Lacey could see and feel me.

"Mom," she said, "I am so glad you're here. I heard Grandma saying some sort of ... something like she had taken over your body. I didn't know ... I'm hoping for an explanation or something."

"I don't know. I thought it was you. It sounded like you, looked like you, and said, 'I am here now, Mom, you can leave.' That soul took over your body," Mom said.

"Yes."

"What happened after she did?"

"She told me I was not needed, that I could vanish."

"Mom, you know better; I would never talk to you like that. Really, Mom, when did I ever ask you to vanish?"

"Come to think of it, you never did."

"Then what happened?"

"She dressed and went down."

"I see. Mom, don't distress yourself. I will figure it out ... I hope."

"You have to locate your father and tell him everything. He might know what to do in this situation."

"All right. I'll do that."

"Lacey, call you father, and tell him to come home. If he asks for me, make up an excuse. Also, inform Gabriellele and Azalea about this."

"On it."

"By the way, where is Gabriellele?"

"She is trying to find out who has taken your place."

"I am going to find Babushka and see if he can help me with this."

"Please call Greg and tell him to come over pronto and observe. I do not want any of you guys taking any chances with this; just go and do your usual things as you normally would."

"Mom, what about Melisa and Cameron?"

"Don't tell them anything. Just watch for them; if you mention it to Melisa, she will overreact, and she will act different. That might aggravate the entity."

"Viktoria, Brandon just pulled into the driveway. He is going to feel the difference between her and you."

"We will find out now. I'm going to go downstairs. Lacey, you stay here."

"Viktoria, I'm home!"

"I was worried about you, darling. Where were you?"

"I can't believe this! Now you're pretending nothing happened?"

"I am sorry, Brandon. Let's not go through this again; I'm tired, and I want to go to bed."

"What the hell happened to you? Were you hit by a spirit or something? You never give up a fight that fast! I know you have something planned; otherwise, you would not be this calm." He sighed. "Go ahead; go to bed. I will be up soon. First, I want to check on Mom."

"She is fine! Don't disturb her."

"I just want to see her."

"Honey, I just told you that she's fine. I checked up on her before; she's sleeping."

"Who is she, Mom?" I asked, when I knew Brandon couldn't hear me.

"I don't know, Viktoria. I have to find your dad."

"Someone is in the driveway."

"Must be Greg."

"Lacey called him and told him your father was here. He has to stay in this house overnight."

"All right, Mom."

"Hi, Uncle Greg," Lacey said as she answered the door. "Mom said you have to find a reason to stay overnight here to find out who has taken over her body."

"Don't worry, Lacey. I will tell your father that pipes are broken and my house is flooded and Viktoria said to come over and stay until the water is drained out."

"You are a genius, Uncle Greg!"

"Where is your mother now?"

"She is right next to me."

"Viktoria, how did this happen? You did not listen to any warnings. Why did you not have Shia stand by? He would have at least protected you and stopped the other soul from taking over!"

"I did! But the soul I had watching me was my mother, and the entity parroted me so Mom released my body to it."

"How long were you out of your body?"

"Good four hours."

"Viktoria, you know better than that! You can only leave the body for at most two hours!"

"Well, Babushka told me to return, but I was more occupied with

Brandon. I had to find out who the demon was that was following him and why."

"I suppose you never heard the saying 'curiosity killed the cat'?"

"This did not kill me, but it took my body!"

"What about your father?"

"I have not see him yet."

"Greg, you go inside and try to find out what is going on."

"Where is Brandon now?"

"He is in Mom's room."

"How is the other soul reacting to the change?"

"Unfortunately too well."

"Viktoria, if I were you, I would be worried Brandon might decide to keep the other you."

"How can you be so flippant, Greg?"

"I would have loved to have been here when the other Viktoria was so nice to your Brandon!"

"Don't forget, Greg, that payback is a big capital B! Did you ever think about doing stand-up instead of being a demonologist? You seem to be doing a good job," I said sarcastically.

"All right, calm down. I still believe you should think about what I said."

"You could not be funnier."

"Viktoria," Mom said, "he is right. If we cannot get her to release your body, what are you going to do? What about the kids? What would they do without you? God, I do not want to think about this; it's so horrible!"

"I will hang around you and Babushka. This is like the old days!" I said, referring to when my parents were still alive.

"Oh no, baby, do not joke about that. We need to consume some energy. I'm sorry."

"Are you rejecting my offer, Mom?"

"No, baby, just trying to keep your spirits up."

"Thanks, Mom. I've had my share of exasperation today!" I said with a smile.

"I see mother and daughter bonding."

"Oh my God, Babushka! I am so happy to see you!"

"Why are you out of your body?"

"Well, we don't know how to explain …"

"You mean you do not know how to describe, Viktoria."

"I was here observing everything and trying to figure out this problem that you have created."

I saw Greg coming back. "Do you know who the soul is that has taken over my body?"

"Not yet, Viktoria, but we will find out."

"Greg, you're going to have to try to keep Brandon away from her. Make sure they do not sleep in the same bed!"

"How am I going to do that?"

"I am sure you will find a way. Let Brandon go to sleep. Ask … Viktoria to stay up. Tell her … that it's important and that you need to talk to her now."

"Let's go in."

"I do apologize for imposing on you and Viktoria, Brandon, but the pipelines in my house are busted. The whole house is flooded, and I called Viktoria to ask her if I could stay the night. She said it was okay to stay for a few days."

"That's fine, Greg," Brandon said. "But Viktoria did not mention anything."

"It must have slipped out of my mind; I completely forgot about Greg," said the fake Viktoria.

"Oh, no, Babushka!" I said. "Nelly is coming out of her room!"

"It's okay, Viktoria, just go and try to whisper in her ear. She can hear you; tell her a lost soul has taken over your body, that that thing is not you."

"Is she going to understand that, Babushka? I don't want to scare her."

"Viktoria, do as I am asking you to; she will understand."

I went to Nelly's room. "Nelly, can you hear me?"

"Yes, Viktoria, where are you?" she said, standing next to the door.

"I'm right next to you, but you cannot see me. I was doing out-of-body traveling, but unfortunately, another soul has taken over me."

"Are you telling me that that body is yours, but the soul is not? Is that why you have been acting strange?"

"Yes. Why, what did she do?"

"She came into my room earlier, looked at me, and said, 'Do you know who you're dealing with?'

"When I said, 'Are you okay, Viktoria?' she said, 'How about calling me Lilin from now on?'"

*Oh my God!* I said to myself. *Who is Lilin?* But I did not want to worry Nelly, so I said, "Not to worry. I will be back in my body as soon as we get a chance. When everything is ready, Greg will inform you of what you have to do. Just listen to him."

Someone knocked on the door. A second later, Greg walked in. "Good evening, Greg," she said like she had no idea why he was there but was pleased nonetheless. "I thought I heard your voice. How are you?"

"I am just fine."

"Ma … Nelly, did we disturb your sleep?"

"No, dear, arthritis pain will not let me sleep at night. I need to get up and take my medicine. That may help me to sleep."

"Viktoria, since when do you call Nelly, 'Ma'?" asked Greg.

"Did I say 'Ma,' Nelly? I didn't even realize that. I'm so exhausted; it's been a long night."

"I need to talk to you about this case; something came up. It's important that we agree on it, Viktoria."

"Well, people, if you have work to discuss, don't let me keep you away from it; I'm going to bed."

"Not so fast," Greg said to Nelly. "As I said, after we finish with the work, which Viktoria has not even looked at since you got sick—"

"Greg, can't we do this tomorrow? I'm tired; I can barely concentrate on work right now."

"It won't take long. I have some pictures I want you to see; it's very important. I had some clients come in who think that their daughter has been possessed by a demon. Lately, she's been acting strange, they said, and she has been practicing rituals in the middle of the night."

"So? There is nothing wrong with people worshiping Lucifer; what can we do?"

"They're asking for advice from me. I told them to go and consult an imam; he might be able to do an exorcism."

"So you told them that there is nothing else we can help them with?"

"Maybe not, but they have something. They just need help."

"Zahra keeps mentioning Lilith and Samuel. Also, her birthday matches the others, and she is still alive! We can bring her over to the United States!"

"I don't think she will make it over here. Lilith or Samuel will be vanquishing her soon. It's too late for that."

"Babushka, did you find out who she is, and why she is here? Who sent her over here?"

"Viktoria, I believe she is Lilin, the daughter of Lilith and a jinn, who takes the form of a beautiful woman to seduce men. Lilith and Samuel sent her."

"What did you say?"

"That's what Nelly told me when she went to her room; she said, 'How about calling me Lilin from now on?'"

"Samuel and Lilith. Apparently, Brandon turned against them."

"Babushka, you're going too fast. What are you telling me?" I asked.

"Brandon had a deal with them. He did not know that they wanted him to pay the consequences."

"Babushka, what kind of a deal could Brandon have made with them? He is going to worship them?"

"I don't know, baby, but this has been going on for a long time. And he did not keep to his end of the bargain."

"You know, Babushka, you can be convincing. I've heard that name Samuel before." I thought about it for a second before I remembered where I had heard it. "Yes, Gabriellele heard Brandon talking to someone named Samuel, and when I asked, he mumbled something about one of his a co-worker Samuel calling about his patients."

"Something is either threatening Brandon to find out what he has done or end him. He must be a threat to them."

"Babushka, we have to stop them! You have to do something!"

"Don't worry, Viktoria. Everything is under control. Just do not underestimate Lilin. She can be a force; after seducing Brandon, she could kill him. We have to be extra careful."

"As long as she is in your body, she can harm you as well as Brandon and the kids."

"What are you saying?"

"She is here to finish all by seducing Brandon and killing the rest of the family."

"Are you saying what I am thinking?"

"Calm down, Viktoria; don't make matters worse."

"How can you tell me to calm down? How are we going to stop her? What happens if she goes upstairs and tries to seduce him and Brandon has no idea that she is not me? Babushka, we have to tell him somehow!"

"No, Viktoria, we cannot mention anything to Brandon. The only thing we need to do is get him out of here. You need to talk to Greg and somehow get Brandon out of this house!"

"Okay, Greg, we need to get Brandon out of the house. It is Lilin who has taken over my body. Lilith and Samuel sent her over to punish him for not keeping his end of the deal. So they have decided to use my body and finish it all—Brandon and whoever is in this house."

"What does this mean?"

"Once she is done with my body, I naturally will take over, and when the cops find me, I will be covered with my family's blood. And you know the rest."

"Oh my God, Viktoria, we have to stop them now!"

"Please go into Nelly's room, and tell her to call Brandon and ask him to take her to the hospital since she is not feeling well. Whatever you do, don't mention what I told you."

"All right, I'll do it. But what if Lilin realizes something is going on? Would that be dangerous?"

"Act normal. Don't let her think otherwise. Go and tell Nelly so she will know."

He went to her room and knocked on the door. "Nelly, are you sleeping?"

"No, Greg, I am still waiting for the medicine to do its trick. Come in. Is there something wrong?"

"Yes. We have to get you and Brandon out of this house."

"Why? What's wrong?"

"Please, Nelly, don't ask anything. I may not be able to answer it."

"Okay. Is it something to do with that soul taking over Viktoria's body?"

"Yes, but we have to hurry."

"What would you like me to do?"

"Call for Brandon. When he comes down, act as though you cannot breathe and say your chest hurts."

"Would she believe that? The other Viktoria, I mean."

"Yes, I think so. But that is why we want you to get Brandon out of this house, just in case."

"I will try my best, Greg."

"As soon as I go into the kitchen, call Viktoria. She thinks I am in the kitchen."

When Greg came into the kitchen, Nelly yelled out, "Viktoria? Do you think you can call Brandon downstairs for me? I do not feel good; I'm having a problem with my breathing. Also my chest hurts."

"You will be fine; you are just tired. Try to sleep."

"No, really, I think I should be taken to the hospital."

"If you feel that bad, I should call an ambulance."

"I think you should. I think I need to go to the hospital!"

"Let me get him right away, Nelly."

She ran upstairs and shook Brandon awake. "Brandon, get up! Your mom is not feeling well! She has a pain in her chest! I called the ambulance already. We need to take her to the hospital fast!"

Brandon immediately started putting his shoes on. "All right, coming down right away. Tell her not to panic."

"Is everything okay, Viktoria?" Greg asked, trying to be convincing.

I, personally, thought he wasn't pulling it off enough, but the other Viktoria must have believed him since she said, "No, not really. Nelly is having chest pains. Brandon and I are taking her to the hospital."

"I will go with Brandon," he said as he put down his cup of coffee. "Viktoria, you stay with the kids. So when they get up, you'll be here to comfort them."

Brandon ran into his mother's room, coat already on. "Mom! Come on, let's go! I called Justin; he's waiting for us at the hospital."

"Wait, Brandon, I'm coming with you; you may need help."

"No, it's okay, Greg. Stay. I'll be fine," he said as he got his mother ready to leave.

"Are you sure, Brandon? You might want some company."

"I'm sure. Viktoria, you stay. If I need anything, I'll call you. Plus, the kids are sleeping; when they get up, I don't want them to panic."

"All right. Then give us a call when you know something."

After they left, Greg turned to Viktoria. "You know what? I'll just put tea on. Would you join me for a nice cup of tea, Viktoria, while we are waiting for them?"

"Why not?" she asked with a smile. "I can't do anything right now, anyway. Let me get the tea bags. I believe there is a pound cake here, too, if you feel like a slice."

"No, just tea will be fine. You should sit down; I can get it. Do you take milk, sugar, or lemon?"

"Just lemon."

"Greg," I whispered, "when you get the chance, there are sleeping pills in the upper cabinet. Grab a couple."

"Okay, but why?" he whispered back.

"Babushka said once she has fallen asleep, take her upstairs and tie her down onto the bed so she can't fight back."

"Did you say something?" the other Viktoria asked. "Is everything okay over there, Greg? Do you need help?" When he shook his head no, she sighed. "I hope Brandon calls soon."

"Here comes the tea. It might relax us a bit. We need it. Did you call Brandon yet to see if they made it to the hospital?"

"No, I have not. I'm waiting for him to call."

"You look tired and worn-out. Maybe you should take a rest."

"You're right; I'm just tired. The tea you made really did relax me. Thank you, Greg. I am glad you are staying." She started to get up. "I cannot wait for Brandon's call." She gave a yawn. "I'm going to sleep. Would you wake me up when he calls? I need to tell him something, but I did not get the chance."

"If you want," Greg said, playing with the string of his tea bag, "I can go to the hospital and stay with Nelly. He could come home. Would you like that, Viktoria?"

"We will wait until he calls. I would not mind a second cup of tea, but this time, put extra mint liqueur in it. It's a very tasty tea. Brandon might call by then."

A while later, Greg said, "Viktoria, I am worried. It has been more than two hours. Brandon still has not called; I think I should go."

"You're right. I'm worried too. If you should go there, the key—in case I fall asleep—is under the mat outside the door. I don't think Brandon took his house key either; he was in such a rush."

"I am going to the hospital to see if everything is okay. Meanwhile, you go get some rest, Viktoria. We have a long day tomorrow."

After Greg left, she went upstairs, but I did not follow her. Five minutes later, I said, "Babushka, Greg is waiting two houses down. Has Lilin gone to bed yet?"

"Not yet, but she is about to. My concern is she suspected something; if she did, this could turn against us."

About forty-five minutes later, Lilin fell asleep.

"Viktoria," Babushka said, "go get Greg. Lilin is in a deep sleep. Just be careful that she doesn't sense your presence."

"Greg, come back. Babushka thinks Lilin has gone into a deep sleep. Just keep it low, so she doesn't wake up."

"Okay, Viktoria, I have the keys. Is the alarm on?"

"No, it's not. I am the only one who knows the code. It's impossible for her to put it on. Let's go in."

"Viktoria, I'm going to need Lacey to help me. Is she up?"

"Yes, Greg, Lacey's waiting for you. She has the Bible and the cross, as well as the holy water. You need to tie Lilin down first; she might harm you."

"All right, Viktoria. I have the handcuff ready. Is Babushka in the room? I need his help as well."

# Chapter 11

## *My Own Exorcism Experience*

"Greg, everyone's there, waiting for you."

As Greg took one of her hands to tie it as tightly as he could to the bedpost, Lilin woke up. I could tell that she was very strong.

Greg decided to do the exorcism as soon as he could and not wait for the priest. As a demonologist, he had performed exorcisms many times before.

As Lilin strained to break free, Greg recited a prayer. "All-powerful God, all the sins of your unworthy servant. Give me constant faith and power, so that armed with the power of your holy strength, I can attack this cruel, evil spirit in confidence and security ..."

Lilin was getting very restless. She started hissing, shaking the bed, and saying, "You cannot stop Lilith! Sooner or later, Lilith will get what she wants!" Then she turned her head to the side. She knew I was there. She looked at me and said, "Do you want this body in one piece? You had better stop him right now!"

I was petrified. When she said that, for a second, I thought about stopping Greg before she did something really horrible. I even said, "Stop, Greg! She is going to hurt my body! Please stop!"

"Viktoria," he said, not even bothering to look my way, "don't believe her. We have to go through with this. Don't listen to what she is saying. This is the only way."

Greg then continued on, "I exorcise you, Most Unclean Spirit! Spirits! Of Lilin! In the name of Our Lord Jesus Christ, be uprooted and expelled from this creature of God … I command you to leave Viktoria's body."

This was taking forever. Lilin would not give up the fight. She started to scrunch up her face and kept saying, "Stop this, or I will destroy the body and Viktoria will never be able to use it again! It will be the end of her. What will you say to her kids and her husband? I killed your mother?"

Greg was stopping, but Babushka told him not to. I felt my heart breaking for Lacey, who was watching my body and telling Lilin, "You have to give my mom's body back! Don't hurt her!"

"I don't want Brandon coming home anytime soon. I hope Nelly will be able to keep him there longer."

Greg made the sign of the cross on my forehead and pressed a relic against my chest as he finished the exorcism with: "Go away, Seducer! Hell is your home. The serpent is your dwelling. Be humiliated and cast down. Even though you have deceived men, you cannot make a mockery of God … time has prepared hell for you and your mother, Lilith, and your father, Lucifer, and their demons."

He looked up at me. "Viktoria, stay next to your body. As soon as she is out, just flow back into your body—but only when I say, 'Now.'"

As I waited anxiously for Greg to say the word, I could see Lilin almost giving up. Greg kept repeating the verse until finally, Lilin left my body. I heard Greg say, "Now!" but Lilin heard him too and jumped right back in to fight back; she laughed with her crushed voice. Lilin started to become more aggressive; it was becoming impossible, and Babushka told Greg to stop until we could get help from the elders. Meanwhile, we had to think of a way to keep Brandon in the hospital longer. As we were discussing a strategy, the priest came. Greg and Father Wilson started the exorcism over, and I asked Lacey to leave the room and stay with her siblings. It was taking too long, and it did not look good.

I heard Gabriellele yelling, "The basement! The basement!" repeatedly. "There is something in the basement!" she screamed.

Things started to get out of control, and I went to the stairs to see what was going on. As I was trying to listen, I saw Lilith and Samuel rushing up to my room.

Babushka met Lilith and Samuel by the door.

"Do be careful!" I tried to warn them.

"Victoria, the elders are here. We want you to get back to your room."

I heard Lilith demanding that they let Lilin go; otherwise, she would use her power to destroy the children.

I could see the elders, and I heard them ordering Lilith to take all her demons and her daughter. There was some sort of white light mixed in with a cloud. Lilith looked scared.

"I will go, but I promise I will be back," she said, and then she looked at me and said, "You will be sorry and vanquished. You will pay for this!"

"Now, Viktoria! Just flow in."

As soon as I had taken over my body, Greg sprayed it with holy water to see my reaction. He placed the cross on my forehead to make sure it was me. I heard Lacey saying, "Welcome back, Mom!" I could not believe how close I had been to becoming a lost soul.

"It's good to be back, Lacey. Thank you, Greg and Father Wilson, for what you have done. Thank you so much. I can't ever repay you."

"Viktoria, how do you feel? We have to clean the scratches. They're still bleeding."

"I'm fine, Greg. I just feel a bit tired, and my face is burning hot." I looked up and saw my father. "Babushka, I'm glad you're here. I need your help. You know more than you have told me."

"Viktoria," Greg said, interrupting. "I'm going over to the hospital. I'll let Nelly know everything is okay and that they can return to the house."

"You don't need to, Greg. She has been informed; they should be home soon."

"Viktoria," Greg said, "get yourself cleaned up and try to think of some sort of explanation for what happened and how your face got scratched."

As soon as I got up to get cleaned up, Brandon called.

"Hi," I said after I answered. "I was worried sick! Why did it take you so long to call, Brandon? How is Nelly doing? Is she staying in the hospital?"

"Mom is fine. She just had a side effect from the medicine she has been taking. Justin thinks she also had an anxiety attack due to the medicine. We are on our way home."

"Okay then, I'll see you soon." When I hung up, I turned to my daughter. "Lacey, go to your room and pretend you are sleeping. Greg, get those blankets and lie down on the couch. I'm going to clean up. Greg, could you also open the door when they get here? When Brandon asks me what happened, I will tell him I heard noises and went outside to check it out. When I saw two raccoons, I panicked and fell down in the bushes."

"Do you think he's going to buy that, Viktoria? Brandon will start to investigate; you know how he is."

"Don't worry, Greg. A few days ago, Brandon did see a raccoon in our backyard, so he will buy that. He even said to be careful when I take out the garbage."

"I think they're here. Don't you think you should go upstairs and clean up?"

I ran upstairs and into the bathroom. The scratches weren't too bad, but I didn't think I'd ever be able to wear this shirt again. It was completely ruined with blood.

I heard Greg open the door. "Hey, thanks, Greg," I heard Brandon say. "Where's Viktoria?"

"She's upstairs getting cleaned up. There was a little accident."

"What happened? Is she okay?"

"Yes, she is. Don't worry; it was only a little mishap. She has some scratches that need to be cleaned up; that's all. So how do you feel, Nelly? You gave us quite a scare. However, you look much better than before."

"Yes, I am. Doctor Justin said that it was a side effect of the medicine, but I'm fine now. I'm so sorry to scare you all. I'm going upstairs to check on Viktoria and see how bad the little incident was. Oh! There she is now!"

"Are you okay, honey?" Brandon asked, deeply concerned. "You look like you have been wrestling!"

"I'm fine, Brandon. I heard noises outside and went to check it out. I went to the side of the house where the noises were coming from. I did not see anything, but as I turned my back, I saw the two raccoons just looking at me with curious eyes. I panicked and fell on the rosebushes." I knew lying wasn't right, but if he were to get involved, it would be much worse. I was sorry, but I felt I must.

"Wow, Viktoria, that looks bad. Did you use antiseptic to clean it so it will not get infected? I told you to be careful! I told you there were raccoons! But you still went outside in the dark." He shook his head. "I don't know what to tell you, Viktoria." He gave a little smile before kissing me on the forehead. "Okay, people, I'm going to bed now. I have an early morning, so see you all later."

"Okay, honey. You go. I'll be up soon." Once he was gone, I turned to Nelly. "So, how do you feel, Nelly?"

"Good."

"Thank you so much, Nelly, for getting Brandon out of the house. I'm sorry you had to lie to him; I know you do not like lying."

"That's okay Viktoria. How are you doing? This is you, right? It's not the other soul? This is must be you because the other soul looked mean, and her eyes were like cat eyes."

"Yes, it is me, Nelly, not the other soul. I'm fine apart from the scratches, which Lilin left."

"Well, if you're okay, I think I will be going to bed now, even though I took a little nap at the hospital. I need more, so good night, dear, and, Greg, see you in the morning."

"All right, then I'm going to bed as well. Greg, if you need more covers just get them from the closet by the steps."

"I am okay with these. Listen, Viktoria, we need to talk to my friend about a young woman who needs help."

"Sure. As soon as I get the kids out of the house, we will talk, but for now, good night."

It had been a long, seemingly endless night. I felt tired and sore, but it was good to have my body and family back. That was a terrifying experience that I did not wish to go through again. I would have to be more careful when doing astral travel.

"Viktoria," Brandon said as he crawled into bed, "you wanted to discuss something with me before. What was it? You said it was important."

"Never mind, go to sleep; I already forgot what it was," I lied. The other Viktoria had wanted to talk to him, not me.

I was so proud of Lacey. She was such a natural; I knew she would do well in life. She kept commanding Lilin with such force, and it was her first psychic experience!

After the whole event, I had trouble sleeping. Those "what-if" questions kept running through my mind. For instance, what if I had been unable to resume my body? What if it had taken Greg much longer to work it out? What if Brandon had come home in the middle of it?

Babushka always told me how this could seriously cause harm to a person and his or her family. I would have to do this again with Alia and the others to find her twin brother, but next time, I would have extra protection.

The next day, I got up and tried to think of what to say if Brandon asked me the question that I had been able to dodge the night before. Luckily, he didn't. Everyone left after breakfast. I knew that Nelly wanted to tell me something, but I thought that Brandon should be with me when she did.

"How are you doing this morning, Nelly?" I asked when I walked into her room. She was lying on the bed, reading the paper, which one of the kids must have gotten for her. "Did you get any sleep? I do apologize for what happened; it was out of my control."

"Oh dear, don't worry. As long as we have you back! It's okay; this is your work. You have been given a wonderful gift; you should be using it, even though it has difficulties."

"I wish Brandon was as understanding as you. Well, he used to be, but since I took on this case, I don't know." I shrugged. "I don't even know him anymore."

"Well, dear, he's probably having a hard time at work with his new deals and with the hospital. Perhaps he's just confused. Justin will be stopping by in a few days to see me. I believe he has some pictures to show you."

"That would be nice. I wonder what kind of pictures though."

"Well, he said something about how he was right and he has the pictures to prove it."

"Well, Nelly, I don't recall anything about pictures, but we will find out when he gets here."

For the next few days, I didn't mention anything about my work to Brandon. I pretended that everything was fine and that nothing had happened. Meanwhile, he was under the magnifying glass; Gabriellele, Azalea, and my babushka were watching him, following him every step he took. I did not want him to be hurt by Lilith or any kind of entity. I had some kind of hunch he might be the worshipper. God, I hoped I was wrong.

I just really hoped I was wrong.

"Nelly," I said a couple of days later, "I need to drop off some files with Michael. Then I'll stop by Greg's; it's about a client, but it shouldn't take long. Do you think you'll be okay for few minutes by yourself?"

"Of course, I will be fine. The nurse should be here soon, so don't worry. Do what you need to do."

"I know Justin is stopping by today, but I will be back before he gets here. If he comes before I do though, please tell him to wait for me. I am dying to see the pictures!"

Just as I was about to leave, the doorbell rang. I was hoping that it would be the nurse, so that I did not have to leave Nelly alone. Fortunately, it was Michael.

"God, Michael, I'm so glad to see you! I was just about to leave and drop off the files for you. Then I was planning to stop by Greg's. I believe he said something about a friend of his having problems with an exorcism, if I remember right."

"Well, good thing you did not just speak to Greg. He's supposed to stop by over here. He should be coming soon." He looked over his shoulder and nodded at the driveway. "Look, Doctor Justin just drove in. I thought it would be an inconvenience for you to come to the office, so I came to pick up the files and see how Nelly was doing."

"Well, that's nice of you. Please, come in. Nelly is in her room; she should be out soon." I wanted Justin to get out of his car and come to the door. When he was close enough, I said, "Hi, Justin. Good to see you. I'm dying to see what you are about to show me." I looked up at his face and was taken aback by what I saw. "What's wrong? You look like you just killed a patient of yours."

"Well, Viktoria, it may be worse than that. If Nelly had not talked me into it, I would have kept myself out of this, but I hope I that am doing the right thing."

"What is it, Justin? What happened?"

"We're both under the obligation ..." He trailed off and then said, "Viktoria, let's wait for Nelly."

"I could leave," Michael volunteered. "I can get the files later since this seems like it might be personal."

"Don't leave, Michael," Justin said. "This is something you should be hearing as well. It concerns Viktoria and maybe the case you're both working on."

"Are you sure, Justin?" Michael then turned to me. "If you want me to leave, I will. You just tell me later."

"There she is," I said to Justin. I put my hand on Michael's arm. "Stay. I think I know what they are going to tell me. I would like you to stay and hear it. Let me start the conversation; first, Justin, is it about my twins?"

"Yes, Viktoria, it is. At first, I did not know how this happened, and whatever we tell you, don't hold anything against Nelly or me. We have tried to keep it to ourselves, but as things were getting worse with Nelly, I decided to tell you; it's probably the right time."

"Yes. Nelly, you're going to be okay. Just tell me. Last time ... well, you know what occurred. I don't want you to get sick again. Do you want Brandon here with us or would you to rather tell me first?"

"I don't think it would be a good idea to have Brandon with us until I tell you what I overheard. We will both need answers from Brandon. Why would he do such an unthinkable thing?"

"Can someone start talking?" Michael said angrily. "I'm going insane over here trying to figure out what is going on!"

"My dear," Nelly said, leading me to the couch and sitting down. "Right before you got pregnant and married, do you remember that Brandon was offered a position out of nowhere? The best position a person could have? He had just completed his internship, but somehow, he managed to get that job. Do you remember that? Then the other case, with the law firm? It was just before you had the twins."

"Yes, I do remember. I even talked about it with Michael and Greg. It came up during our investigation of a person who used to be an intern in that firm."

"Well, Brandon was practicing some kind of unknown black magic and recruiting people into it—all for his success and power— until they demanded something more than he bargained for. At first, he thought he would have to go through with it."

"What was the demand? Nelly, what is it that was so easy and unthinkable that he has done?"

"I don't know how to tell you. When I heard what he had done, I could not believe it. At first, I thought it was some kind of sick joke! Brandon could not have done this! It was impossible!"

"How did you find out about it? Who told you?"

"Viktoria, I will tell what I know first and then Nelly can tell you the rest. It would be for the best, if it is okay with you. I want you to take a deep breath and take your medicine, Nelly. You don't look well."

# Chapter 12

## *Twins*

"That night, when the twins were born ... you know how crazy it was there," Doctor Justin said. "There was a baby boy stillborn, and right in the middle of the birth of the twins, I was called for another emergency. That was when I thought my daughter was missing. Brandon told me go to ahead and do what I felt like needed to be done. There was a practitioner who helped you with the birth. I believe her name was Leila. Yes, that was the name Brandon told me. I do remember that very clearly; Brandon was trying to get me out of the room for some reason. However, I did hear the nurse telling Brandon that it was a baby girl and a baby boy. When they took the babies out of the room, I picked them up to take a closer look at them. Nurse Kelly happened to have a camera right then, and I asked her to take a picture of the twins and me, so she did.

"The next day, I came to see how the twins and you were doing. Right before I could see you, there was an announcement calling me to an emergency. I never got the chance to see you afterward because I was transferred to another state—at Brandon's request; he said this would be better for my career, running a brand-new hospital by myself. Yes, I took the job, but I did not join them, even though many times I came close to it; what they offered was unbelievable. So, I continuously kept in touch with Nelly, and she told me about what she had overheard. That was when I understood why they were trying to keep me out of it. Nelly and I put the pieces together. If you check the name tags on their wrists, they have your name and their gender.

"Later that day, I checked the file for the births of twin baby boys, and then I inspected the death of twin baby boys. The file on you and twin boys did not exist."

"Justin, what are you telling me?" I asked, not believing what was right in front of me. "How could they lose the file? It has to show me as a patient at least! Who was the female doctor? I do not even remember seeing any female doctors during the birth that night. What did you say her name was? Leila? I believe it was Leila who was trying to keep you away for the kids' safety. I suppose they would not want you or your family to get hurt over this. That was why they sent you away, Justin."

"Together, we have tried to figure out what Brandon has done."

"I have a question for you," Michael said to Doctor Justin from his seat on the chair across from me. "If they are alive, where is the boy? I believe I know where the girl is, but I need to find out about the boy. It's very important."

"I do know where the boy is. He knows who you are. He is a very fine young man."

"Where he is? I have to know. I don't know if I should be mad, angry, or frustrated with you all!" I sighed before I continued, "But I'm glad you told me that they are alive. Just take me to them, Justin, right now. I will deal with Brandon later. I'm convinced what he did was wrong, but we will get over this."

"Viktoria, let me call him over. Do you think you're ready for this right now?"

"Yes, I am ready. I can't tell you how grateful I am to you and Nelly." I turned to my mother-in-law. "Nelly, I'm not upset or hurt, so I don't want you to blame yourself for anything. You had a reason for what you did, I understand. Remember that I love you; I will never be upset with you. I want you to understand."

"Oh dear, I don't know how can I make it up to you. I am full of regret."

"I don't want you to feel that remorsefulness ever. Whatever it is, tell me. How did you find out?"

"It was your father and mother who told me before their accident, God rest their souls. They knew they wouldn't be back, so your mom asked me to keep an eye on you and the kids. After all, no matter what age you are, you still need a mother. Your dad told me when things got complicated, I should tell you what I know. He also told me you would understand. I believe your dad had also spoken to Justin as well."

*Thanks, Babushka! That's good timing; as I promised, I would never do anything to hurt Nelly's feelings. I care so much for her, just like I still care for you and Mom,* I thought in my head.

"Michael," I asked out loud, "can you go pick up Alia and bring her over here?"

"Justin, can you call ... my son ... and ask him to meet us over here. Tell him to be careful. What is his name, Justin?"

"Oh, yes. It's Damien." He must have seen the shock on my face, because he continued, "I told you that you have met him, and he did take care of Grandma Nelly."

"Oh my God! Just the other day, I was thinking about how much he looked like Brandon! The way he stood and spoke—even his eyes are like Brandon's. But he said his mother was sick."

"Yes, Viktoria, his adoptive mother. She passed away the day before."

"Nevertheless, how am I going to explain to him about us? I don't know; do you think he will reject us? What happens if he doesn't want to see me? If he thinks—"

"Viktoria, calm down. He knows everything, so don't worry. His adoptive parents told him, and he has been waiting for me to call him. He knows. We'll be having these discussions with him."

"I have a question," Michael said to me. "What am I hearing? Are these the twins we have been looking for? Isn't, perhaps, Alia your girl?"

"Yes, yes, Michael, go get Alia and call Greg. Tell him what is going on; he has to be here. Don't worry; you have protection with you. I see Babushka and Gabriellele." Once he left to get Alia, I turned to everyone else. "I am sure Alia knows about this too. That is why Brandon was there watching her, and then when he saw Damien, he looked like he'd seen a ghost. Brandon did not want me to find out." I picked up my phone. "My dear Brandon," I said sarcastically as I dialed his number, "you're about to have the worst nightmare you've ever had."

"Hi, honey," I said when he picked up. "I know you're busy; I won't take up much of your time. It's just that Justin is here to see how Nelly is doing, and we were talking about you. We remembered your birthday is in two days, so we decided to celebrate tonight. It's Friday, and everyone is free, so what do you think?"

"That's okay with me. If Mom is feeling better, then why not? But, honey, I will be an hour late. Is that okay?"

"Yeah, that's fine. We'll meet you at your favorite restaurant then. I have a surprise for you as well." Then I hung up.

"Justin, call your wife. We're all going out tonight to celebrate Brandon's birthday, even though it's in two days. I want to give him an early birthday present. The best ever: his kids! What do you think, Nelly? Would you say that is the best present?"

"Viktoria, are you okay? I'm concerned about you. It would be the best birthday gift, but instead of you getting mad at him, you're acting as if nothing has happened."

"Nelly, lately, what has been going on with our family? We do not need more drama; I think we've had our share of it. We need to be happy and thankful. I did find my children. I have grieved for them for twenty-seven years. Thanks to Leila and my power-loving husband, my kids are alive today."

Justin then got a call from Damien. He was at the front door. I asked Justin to open the door, since I was nervous as well as anguished. I did not know what to say or how to react. But at the same time, my heart was pounding, and I wanted to hold him. He was my baby, and I had not seen him in twenty-seven years, or at least as my son!

As he was walking in, I watched him and admired the man he had become. Furthermore, I whispered to Leila, "Thank you for what you have done for me." I was sure she heard me.

Leila would not let him out of her sight. I believe I heard her saying, "It was my pleasure."

Damien approached me, just looked at me, and said, "It has been a long time. The day I saw you in the hospital, I wanted to tell you, but I could not because I was not allowed to. Until today."

"Yes, I understand. I'm sorry we've been kept apart from each other. I am so pleased they did; otherwise, you would not be alive today. I am convinced Leila did her best to keep you and your sister alive."

"My sister? You mean Alia? You know about her too? How did you find out?"

"One day, I decided to do an out-of-body experience—I am sure you already know yourself. I followed Brandon, and I saw him a block away. At the corner of the street was Alia. He was observing her. An unknown person was telling Brandon to leave her alone. He was putting her in danger by being there. At first, I did not recognize the person, and then Babushka said, 'That is Quirel, the jinn watching over Alia' and then it clicked."

As I finished telling Damien the story, Greg and Alia walked in. Looking at her face, I saw Alia was relieved and calm. I saw Greg approach at the same time as they did. Everything was happening so fast; I wanted to pinch myself and hoped it was not some sort of setup again.

I heard Gabriellele and Azalea say, "Viktoria, this is not a setup or dream. Be confident of that; we are by the steps, and your father is next to us. Take a look." And when I did, I saw them there.

"I believe everyone knows why we're all here. I, firstly, express gratitude to Nelly and Justin for bringing this to my understanding and thank Leila for keeping them safe. As you all know, the twins I supposedly lost during birth and the next day were apparently saved by Leila. I don't want to go into details; I am sure most of you know why and how. I want everyone to meet me at Brandon's favorite restaurant, Charlie's, this evening to surprise Brandon and celebrate his birthday.

"As of midnight tonight, we have important projects to finish off. We have to rearrange Lilith's, her friend Samuel's, and the jinns' plans."

Greg and Michael looked over at me, confused. Greg said, "Does this mean our search is over? We are actually able to save the rest."

"Yes, Greg, all this time, what we have been through … and it was right under our noses. Whatever has taken place, there was a reason for it, as Babushka always says. Only one thing left, Michael, why did you call me that first night? You said something about feeling Gabriellele's presence. How did you?"

"Well, I want to be honest. It was what Gabriellele had in her hand: a small piece of paper that said, 'Please call Viktoria.' Then she had your business card."

"Do you think I'm going to fall for that? Why didn't you mention that at the beginning of this case?"

"Well, I did not want you to freak out. I knew Brandon would have tried to stop you if I mentioned that."

"Well, we'll see what he's going to do tonight at the restaurant. I cannot wait to see his reaction, and the best part will be at midnight. I know I can rely on you guys. I will need your help. Also, I believe Carmella will be joining us with her baby. She knew my identity."

"Viktoria, you mean it's almost over? I won't believe it until it's past midnight. How are you doing? I cannot believe you have taken it so calmly after all these years."

"I don't know, Greg. I feel happy! I just want to go somewhere and scream as loud as I can to show my happiness as well my frustration."

"You know what? You should go to your favorite place by the beach and get that out of you. You can scream as much as you want to. Let the anger out. You need to do this; take our advice. Go on; you look like you need it."

"No, I cannot yet. The children should be coming in an hour. I need to be here to explain this to them. I don't expect that they will ever comprehend, but I will try without any misapprehension in future. In fact, I should have Brandon do the explaining. How could he explain it to them?

"By looking at Grandma Nelly's face. She looks likes she is apprehensive, as well as happy. I do feel terrible how she has continued to carry this burden for so long; it must have been immeasurable. It's very puzzling but delightful also. I'm concerned about the rest of the children; hopefully, the kids won't have a hard time understanding, and they will welcome their brother and sister. Alia and Damien, come to me." When they did, Doctor Justin turned to me. I said, "They're so understanding, and they're trying to ease my pain. They even made a joke. I know they are special kids just by looking at them."

It was time to pick the children up from school; I requested that Damien and Alia stay over until I came back with Lacey and Cameron.

When I went to Lacey's school, she seemed concerned. She just jumped in and asked, "Mom, why did Michael come and pick up Mrs. Adams from school? Is everything all right?"

"Yes, Lacey, it is. You know better; there is nothing kept from you, right?"

"Right, Mom. So if that's true, then what has been going on? Nana and Babushka told me. When I confronted Mrs. Adams and said that she could be my sister, Mrs. Adams said, 'Wait until it is clarified by your mother.'"

"How long you have known, Lacey? I believe Babushka and Nana have lots of trust in you. Is there anything else that they mentioned about this matter?"

"Babushka has mentioned something about Mrs. Adams also having a twin brother. So that means that I have another brother!"

"I am so proud of you, Lacey! You have known all this time, and yet you kept it a secret. How do you feel about this matter and about your father's involvement in this? Did this issue bother you at all?"

"No, not really, because Babushka said that what Dad did was for everybody's benefit. Otherwise, the twins would have been dead by now. He also told me how special they are. Babushka said that they deserve special siblings like us."

"Well, honey, I hope the rest of them will understand like you. This was easier than I thought."

"Mom, I know Melisa does understand as well, considering that Babushka told us at the same time, but I do not know how Cameron will take it."

"Wait, what was that? What did you say about Melisa? You mean Melisa can sense Babushka's presence as well? Why, I did not recognize that! Since when?"

"Melisa only talks to Babushka. Nana said it's because she does not like contact with the other side, and she is blocking it. Babushka guided her in how to communicate with him."

"Babushka! I know you can hear me. I have not expressed my gratitude to you so frequently, but for what you have done with my kids ... I am so lucky to have parents like you and Mom. Okay, Lacey, here we are. I do not want you to mention anything to Cameron, understand? I want your father to explain it to him slowly. You know he is a very sensitive little boy."

"Okay, Mom. I won't say anything. Can I make a suggestion for Dad? Before he tells Cameron, he had better get him a brownie with ice cream. Then I am sure Cameron will be just fine."

I went over to the school door and waited until he came out. When I saw him, I took his bag and said, "There is my favorite boy! How was your day at school, Cameron?"

"Good."

"Guess what, Cameron? We're going out to your favorite bistro. You know why we are going?"

"What's a bistro? I never heard of it before. How can it be my favorite place? Why are we going over there anyway?"

"Well, Cameron, bistro is another way to say restaurant; some people like to use this phrase."

"Then what is a phrase, Mom?"

Sometimes I have to remind myself that it just isn't worth it to introduce new words to him. "It means an expression, and please do not ask me what an expression is," I said before he could beat me to it. "Tonight, ask your father the meaning of that word."

I cleared my throat. "We're going to a restaurant because Daddy's birthday is coming up in a few days. That's why you're going to make him a birthday card. As soon as we get home, I want both of you to finish your homework. Also, we have company at home so don't try to get out of it. Do we understand each other, people? As soon as you're finished, we will go to the restaurant."

"Who is the company, Mom? Do I know them? Are they coming with us to the bistro? I think I will use the word *bistro* from now on; it's shorter than *restaurant*. What do you think, Mom?"

Those fast-talking commercials have nothing on my son. "Yes, you're right, Cameron. Look, we're home already, but I need to tell you. It is a surprise party for Daddy, all right?" After he nodded, he jumped out of the car and ran to the door. "Cameron! Just calm down! Don't run! You're going to fall and get hurt!"

When we walked through the door, I saw Nelly and Alia bonding. Tears were rolling down from Nelly's eyes, and Alia was soothing her; it was like watching a movie. I did not want to interrupt them, so I quietly went into the kitchen. I saw Cameron already chatting away to Damien and asking him all sorts of questions that no other child would even have imagined. Shortly thereafter, Lacey came back down and gave Mrs. Adams a hug. She said, "Finally, it's over. I can say you are my sister."

The clock was ticking, and my heart was pounding. I started to question myself: How will Brandon react to this? Would he act like nothing had happened and open his arms to them? It would be a very fascinating night.

Alia and Damien left a little while later. We asked them to meet us at the restaurant; I requested that Alia bring her husband.

It was soon time to go, so everyone went out to the car. Melisa called and said she would be a bit late since she had to finish her assignment before she left.

I felt the presence of my mother. "Where are you, Mom? Why will you not show yourself?"

"Baby, I wish you good luck. You will see at the moment that I am a bit emotional, but I do apologize that I did not say anything to you; I hope you understand, baby."

"Yes, Mom, I do. Very well. I just want you to be here with me at all times—and Babushka. Whatever happens, you are both my family, and families are guardian angels. Don't forget."

"Viktoria, don't forget, your Babushka is there already. He is watching over the twins, so relax, baby."

I closed the door and left. It was getting late; I hoped to see Brandon there already. I did not think I would be able to just sit there and wait.

# Chapter 13

## *The Moment of Truth*

As I thought, Brandon was there at the restaurant already waiting for us. Thank you, God! Right next to him was Melisa. For the first time, she managed to make it on time.

Nelly kept looking at me, probably wondering what I was going to say.

"Nelly, I'm fine. What I want you to do is just relax. I will not overreact and make him feel bad. We both know that he will do that himself when he sees the twins."

"Okay, dear. I just do not want anyone to say anything that might hurt someone's feelings; that's all."

We all sat down. Brandon looked happy; I just kept looking at him and wondering why.

After a while, he asked, "Viktoria, why are you staring at me? Are you okay? Is there something wrong?"

"Oh no," I lied. "I didn't even realize that I was staring at you. I'm sorry. I thought I saw something." I waved it off. "Everything's just fine." I picked up my glass and toasted him, saying, "Honey, happy birthday. As they say, I hope you share many happy and healthy years with loved ones."

"Yes, this is the best gift ever, Viktoria. Thank you. Here come Justin and his wife." He was about to get up when he stopped. "Who are those people behind them?"

"They're not strangers, Brandon. I am sure you've met them

before. This is my little surprise to you. Look, Damien is here too! This is going to be one hell of a birthday celebration. Don't you think so, honey?"

"What is the meaning of this, Viktoria?" he almost yelled. "What are you trying to say? I think that you have gone too far with your little psychic friends!"

"Not really, Brandon. What I really want is for you to enjoy your birthday with the family. Alia and Damien are family; you should be very happy to see the twins, don't you think so?"

"Okay, so you found out. You can at least tell me how you found out!"

"Not really, Brandon. I know why you did it, and I am not angry. I am confused but, at the same time, happy. I want you to be happy too. Now you don't have to sneak out and check up on your kids to see if they're okay. Nevertheless, what I want will happen at midnight. You have to join us for a ritual. Is that a deal?" I was upset, I admit, but it was his birthday and I was glad to know my twins had lived. But still, how could he have hidden this? It gave me a feeling of betrayal. It wasn't fair, me not knowing my kids were alive all this time.

"Viktoria, are you sure you know what you're doing? You know how dangerous this will become if Lilith finds out! She will come after us! This means we're asking for trouble, so think about it. Let's not make a harsh decision. It won't be only the twins this time."

"I know what I'm doing. We have to close the door to hell; we will get help. We need to stop her from killing the rest of the six hundred and sixty-three. Are you with me, Brandon?"

"You know the answer, Viktoria. Yes. Just give me an hour; I need to talk about this with Leila."

"No, Brandon. Before that, I think you should talk to Cameron and explain to him what is going on."

"You're right. I should—the sooner, the better."

"Yes, he is a very bright kid; just be prepared for his questions."

"Leila and the elders decided this. We can do this; we just have to join forces. When we get home, you need to read about everything involving Samuel and Lilith. Now go to the kids and enjoy the rest of the night with them and be proud of them. They might not have the power to get rid of Lilith, but they have the power to stop her for now."

Brandon went to the kids and was enjoying their company. He was so happy, and we had a good time. He pulled Cameron off to the side and called Damien to try to explain what was going on to Cameron.

Out of nowhere, we heard Cameron say, "So, Damien, you are my brother? That's why you look so smart, just like me. And, Alia, does that mean I will be in your class when I go to fifth grade? You are my sister. You know that I don't need to do homework?"

"Slow down, Cameron; you have a few years to go."

"Well, I am just thinking about the future, Alia."

"Well, well," said Alia, "Cameron, you should, because I do give lots of homework. If you don't believe me, ask Lacey."

When it was almost ten, we got ready to go and do what needed to be done. My concern at the moment was keeping Nelly and the kids away from home. I could not take them to Nelly's place; she wouldn't be able to protect them. I had to think of something fast. Then I heard Babushka chanting my name.

"Where are you, Babushka?"

"Come outside. We need to talk. Bring Damien and Alia with you. I will tell you where to meet at midnight. "Viktoria, take the rest of the family to Father Walsh's church. He is having a midnight Mass; they have to stay there until everything is over."

I went to Damien and Alia and told them that Babushka wanted to talk to us. We went outside. The first thing we realized was that the sky was orange, red, and blue. It looked like it was in flames.

"Viktoria, as soon as everyone is gathered, there will be a gentlemen who will approach you. He will not speak—only use sign language. Do not talk to him or look in his eyes. Don't worry; he will take you to places where everyone will be safe. Once you get here, there will be five chosen ones waiting for you all."

"You will be there watching over us, right, Babushka? What happens ... I mean, if it is a setup? What are we going to do?"

"Viktoria, I will not be there; I will be with Nelly and the kids at the church. But Leila will be there. Do not forget; don't ask any questions, just go with them for everyone's safety. I don't even know where they will take you. I believe you should take Nelly and the kids to the church now; they are waiting for you over there."

We went inside and got ready to leave. I decided to leave my car at the restaurant and go with Brandon and the kids.

"Viktoria, what's wrong?" Brandon asked. "You look stressed. Is there something I should know?"

"Nothing, Brandon. I just want to get it over and done with. This case, I mean. I want to go back to my normal life as soon as possible. We need to drop off Nelly and the kids at Father Walsh's church for their safety. Babushka will be there watching over them."

"Why isn't Babushka coming with us?"

"They will not let Babushka and Mom be there, because we will be picked up by some elders who are going to wait for another person who is supposed to come. Then they will take us to the place, and we are not supposed to talk to the person or ask anything. Do not stare into his eyes. This is only what Babushka knows, nothing further. They will discover the rest when we get there."

We dropped Nelly and the kids off at the church, and a few minutes later, we met the rest of the people who would be participating. Greg looked nervous, probably because this was his first time. Right after him, Michael, Alia, and Damien showed up. We were all ready, waiting to be picked up. Finally, someone came. His face had a bright light; even in that dark, you could see his face clearly. We all got into his huge limousine. We did not question him, and we tried not to look at him. Otherwise, that bright light would have blinded us.

Everyone was anxious. We were all trying to overcome our anxiety. I was thinking of the consequences—what would be waiting for us when we got there. For a second, I thought I saw something on Michael's face; he looked like he knew what to expect, and his facial expressions confused me. He was so calm. At one point, I witnessed him communicating with the driver.

I asked him if he was okay. He looked like he had seen the driver. Michael responded, "Who is the investigator, Viktoria? It is in my nature to investigate. I suppose I was right."

A few hours later, we got to the destination. When we all got out of the car, there were four elders waiting in robes. We couldn't see their faces, but they were talking. They introduced themselves; their names were Matthew, Leviticus, Daniel, and Exodus. With the elders, there was a priest, rabbi, imam, and Brahman.

Brandon, Damien, Alia, Greg, and I began to walk through the lines. I wondered where Michael was. He had suddenly disappeared. Out of nowhere, Michael appeared wearing white regalia.

"Why are you wearing those things, Michael?"

With a smile, he said, "I will explain once we're in the boat. You don't need to worry right now."

Once we were all in the boat, I could no longer wait for Michael to come explain himself. I went up to him and asked for an explanation.

"What is going on? Why did you put on this regalia, Michael?"

"I am the fifth elder. I know I should have mentioned something earlier, but I could not. Whatever happened up to the present moment ... well, it was all meant to stop Lilith."

"What are we going to do? Why are we doing this in the water?"

"Well, Viktoria, as you know, since we are in the water, we will start our verse. Then Damien, Alia, Gabriellele, Azalea, and Carmella will continue with their verse; once they start, there will be demons trying to escape in between the verses—meaning there will be lightning. That means archangels are hunting them, so they do not conceal themselves in the clouds, and will bring the demons down into the ocean. You have to understand, demons cannot swim, so they will be vanquished forever. Unfortunately, we cannot contain the purge of Lilith, so we will try to close most of the exits from hell."

# Chapter 14

## *Ceremony*

"We're almost there," Michael said. "I would like everyone to put on the ceremonial dresses that are on the seats. I don't want anyone calling out anyone else's name. Brandon, I need you to swallow this little cross. Don't worry; it will dissolve in two days. This is for your own safety. Everyone hold out your right hand and hold on to your religious symbol. Don't let it go; whatever happens, free the left hand, but hold on with the other very tightly to the individual next to you. Everyone has to stay in this ring. Do not move away from it. It may get very dangerous, so hold on to each other. There will be an odor of something burning; ignore it. That will indicate to your family members that someone is in danger. Call for your acting family representative. Prepare not to talk to them or allude to their family names."

Once we were ready, the boat started making circles with the manifestation of the full moon. It made a luminous light; it was the most amazing thing I had ever seen.

The ceremonies began, and we all started with the same verse. The first time, nothing happened. With the second verse, it started to get windy and cold.

At the third verse, it was starting to get ugly. For our safety, Michael suggested that Greg, Brandon, and I go into middle and sit in meditation position. "Whatever happens, do not get up or look to the sky."

All three of us went into the middle of the circle and sat down, our legs crossed in meditation position. We put our heads down, and Michael started the ritual in Italian.

"*Preghiamo: Il Dio di cielo, Dio di terra, Dio degli Angeli, Dio di Archangeli, Dio dei Patriarchs, Dio dei Prophets, Dio dei Apostles, Dio dei Martyrs, Dio dei Confessors, Dio dei Virgins, Dio che ha il potere di dare la vita dopo la morte ed il resto dopo lavoro, perché non ci è altro …*"

I felt someone grabbing and pulling me, and I screamed.

"Are you okay?" Michael asked.

"Yes, I am," I answered, and Michael continued.

"*Dio che Thee e là può essere altro, per l'arte del Thou IL creatore di tutte le cose, visibile Ed invisibile, di cui Del regno non ci sarà conclusione. Prostrate humbly prima del Majesty Glorious di Thy e beseech Thee per trasportarlo da Thy Power da tutta la tirannia degli alcoolici infernal, dai loro snares, delle loro bugie e del loro wickedness furious; deign, il signore di O, per assegnarci Thy protezione potente e per mantenerlo cassaforte e suono. Beseech Thee attraverso Jesus Christ il nostro signore. Amen.*"

Again, I started to feel the grabbing.

"Michael, they're pulling me!"

Michael continued with no response, "*Dagli snares del diavolo, Tutti: Trasportili signore di O. Grant che la chiesa di Thy può servire a Thee nella libertà sicura, Tutti: Beseech Thee, li sentiamo. Deign per schiacciare giù i nemici Della chiesa santa, Tutti: Beseech Thee, li sentiamo. St. Michael il ArchAngel, li difende nel giorno della battaglia; sia la nostra salvaguardia contro il wickedness e gli snares del diavolo. Il DIO di maggio lo rimprova, noi humbly prega e fa IL thou, Principe di O dell'ospite Heavenly, dall'alimentazione del DIO, del getto in inferno Lucifer e di tutti gli altri alcoolici diabolici, che prowl nel mondo intero, cercanti la rovina delle anime. Amen. La maggior parte del cuore Sacred di Jesus. Amen.*"

I did not understand what he was saying, but to my surprise, Brandon did. I asked, "What was he saying? Can you translate some parts for me?"

"Saint Michael the Archangel, defend us in battle—"

"Are you saying Michael is Saint Michael?"

"I don't know, Viktoria."

"Please continue."

"Be our protection against the wickedness and snares of the devil. May God rebuke him, we humbly pray; and do Thou, O Prince of the Heavenly Host, by the Divine Power of God, cast into hell Lucifer and all the evil spirits, who roam throughout the world seeking the ruin of souls. Amen."

After that, all of the prayers were repeated. Now it was getting really bad; I could hear the thunder and see the lightning all around. The sky looked red like a ruby.

Then they repeated the exorcism ceremonies from different religions: Judaism as well as Islam and Hinduism. Each of the religious men repeated it a few times.

At the same time, I started to hear Melisa's voice calling me. "Mom! Help, Mom, help!" I was about to jump up, but Brandon held me down and closed my mouth with his hand.

"Viktoria," Brandon whispered as he grabbed my arm, "it's not Melisa calling you; they are trying to interrupt the ceremony. Don't listen to them."

At one stage, I could no longer help myself; I had to look up at the sky. Looking up into the flames was a horrifying experience. For a moment, I said to myself, "I must be having a nightmare." Finally, it opened, and the water looked like it had been sucked out of the ocean. This, I could tell, was confusing the demons, because they didn't realize that that was the door that came out of the ocean. As they tried to fly between the clouds and hide, lightning was chasing them. They fell back into the traps. There were fireballs thrown by the demons; one almost got me and Brandon, but somehow, Damien threw himself right in front of us and fought back. It just flew back at them; the light protected the boat.

Then Damien started the blessing: *"Blessings delle persone;*

*blessings degli animali; blessings dei posti non indicati per gli scopi sacred ..."*

I was shocked when I heard Damien doing the blessing, but I knew right then my kids had been blessed.

*"Blessings dei posti indicati per gli scopi sacred; blessings delle cose indicate per gli scopi sacred; blessings delle cose indicate per uso ordinario ..."*

When I asked Damien about the blessing, he replied, "I don't know how I knew the blessing; it just came out."

A half hour later, everything had calmed down. The sky looked so peaceful, like a woman after the birth of a child. I was glad everything had gone like it was supposed to.

"Are you okay, Brandon?"

"Yes, Viktoria, I'm just fine, thank you. Now I feel like I am finally free! I can go back to my normal life without any worries!"

"If I were you," Michael said, "I would be more careful. We can never get rid of Lilith, you know, so watch your back."

"Michael, what are you saying? How about the rest of the girls? Are they still in danger?" I asked.

"As of now, they're all safe. But Lilith will try to get back at us for closing the twelve doors to hell. Number thirteen is still open. That is the one she uses. Do not forget that Lilith is the first wife of Adam, so we cannot get rid of her. She is the mother of the demons. She did go against God. Her existence has to be in this macrocosm. I want everyone to be extra cautious. Lilith might be determined to seek revenge! We might still not be safe; she might still be able to hit us when we least expect it. After what we have done, we will be protected, but I do not know for how much longer."

Brandon and I went to the twins. I was so glad that they were all right and back in our life.

Suddenly, I heard voices. It was Gabriellele and Azalea.

"Yes, Gabriellele? Is everything okay?"

"Yes, Viktoria, there is our light. It's time for us to pass over. It's so bright and looks like a rainbow about to appear! There is Leila welcoming us! Azalea and I have to go through the light now. Thank you for all your help, Viktoria. We will be watching over you and your family as you did for us and saved the rest of the six hundred sixty-one. We do thank you all on their behalf."

"No one needs to thank me; I should be the one doing the thanking! Without you and the others, I wouldn't have known of their existence. I do thank you all."

"Viktoria, take a look to your right. Next to Leila is your mom and Babushka. They are there, and they have opened their loving and caring arms to welcome Azalea and me. We are so happy! They're waiting for us! Viktoria, whenever you need our help, just chant our names, and we will be there for you and your family. But don't forget, all levels thirteen and up are still open. Lilith is determined to fight for her beliefs; she won't stop. Just be careful."

Seeing both going through the light was wonderful. It was amazing now that they were free at last.

# Chapter 15

## *Where Is Melisa?*

Just as I was watching them leave, I got a call from Lacey.

"I am calling because we are concerned about everyone, Mom. Is everything okay? There was a storm over here, and Grandma Nelly wants to talk to you."

"Okay, Lacey, put Grandma Nelly on the phone. By the way, is Babushka with you guys?"

"No, Mom. He said he needs to meet Azalea and Gabriellele at the light with Nana. He has not been seen since then, and something else happened."

"What in God's name happened, Lacey?"

"Well, Grandma Nelly will tell you. She does not look well at all, Mom."

"Hi, Nelly," I said once the phone had been passed over. "Is everything okay?"

"No, Viktoria, I was concerned. We had a bad storm over here. I was watching the news, and they said it was not an expected one. They don't know how this happened. There were big, black clouds that just stood over the church. The lightning was incredibly strong! It hit part of the church! A few people got hurt. I think one of them was the bishop. And we cannot find Melisa! Everyone is searching for her. You and the others have to come back! I'm worried."

"Nelly, what do you mean? Melisa is not with you? She must be around there somewhere! That's impossible! She must be helping people. When did you realize she was missing?"

"Right after the lightning hit the church and that black cloud covered the inside of the church. We could not see each other. I believe there was a sound likes birds' wings flapping, but it was inside the church; it was strange. When the clouds were gone, Melisa had disappeared. I've called her name a few times and looked for her, but she did not respond. Then I asked Father Jacob to help me find her, but she's nowhere to be found."

"Okay, Nelly, calm down. I want you to take your medicine and stay at the church with the kids. We are on our way. Don't go anywhere!"

"Michael, something terrible has happened! Melisa is missing!" I looked behind him. "Look out! There is a black mist approaching the boat." I turned back to him. "I just talked to Nelly, and she said that there was a black cloud and lightning hit the church. Also, the clouds went into the church. No one could see each other. Right after that, the cloud disappeared—and she said she thought there were birds' wings flapping—they could not find Melisa. Michael, do you think the demons have taken her to Lilith for revenge? For us closing the doors and killing some of her demons?"

"Yes. You're right. It is Lilith! She's upset. What did Nelly say about the clouds? That's not a cloud; that's black smoke. It's the demons' creation! And that bird sound was the demons also. Yes, they must have taken Melisa, and they're coming over here to warn us that they have her. Get Brandon and Greg in the middle of the circle, and don't move from there until it's safe. They're here for Brandon."

"Where is Brandon?"

"He went downstairs to wash up. Come to think of it, he has been down there a long time."

I ran downstairs, calling, "Brandon! Are you there?" He did not respond to me. "Right now is not the time to joke around, Brandon!" I went to the bathroom door, but it would not open. I ran back to the stairs. "Michael, come down right now! There is something wrong! Brandon won't open the door!"

I banged on the door. "Brandon, open the door! There is a big black mass approaching us! We have to get you in the circle for your safety!"

The door opened. "What is with all the screaming? I was just washing my face."

"Brandon," Michael said, coming down the stairs. "Just run upstairs and stay in the circle. We believe Lilith has sent the demons back. They're appearing as a mist; we have to stay in the circle. The mist has taken Melisa, so run inside the circle."

"What did you say, Michael? What was that about Melisa? Has she been taken by a demon? I thought this was all over! What happened?"

"Brandon, did you swallow the little cross I gave you?"

"No, I did not. I was having a hard time trying to swallow that thing, so I have it in my pocket. Why, Viktoria?"

"You should have. How could you do this? Why didn't you tell us? We would have taken another precaution! Brandon, Michael and the elders believe those demons are telling us to open the door to hell and let them free in exchange for Melisa. There is no time to argue right now. Just get in the middle and do not move from there. Otherwise, someone is going to get hurt."

"Fine, I'm going in the circle, as you say. But I want you all to open those damn doors so they can let Melisa free."

Before we went into the circle, the black mist had taken over all of the boat. Michael and the elders didn't have a chance to say the verse. We could not see each other; the only thing I could hear was Melisa calling us. I knew I should have stopped it when I heard Melisa's voice the first time.

"Mom! Dad! Help! They're taking me somewhere! Please help me! Please help me!"

"It's Melisa calling me! We have to help her, Michael!"

"I can hear her too, Viktoria," Michael said. "Where is Brandon? Weren't you holding on to him?"

"No. Where is he? I did not even get a chance to hold on to him; the mist is so dark I couldn't see him."

"Viktoria, I am here," I heard Brandon say, "but that black mist took Damien. I heard Melisa, and there was something in the mist about to grab me, but Damien jumped in front of me and saved me. They've taken him! We have to get both of them back!"

"Oh, what are we going to do? We need to stop them!"

"Calm down, Viktoria. We will get Melisa and Damien back; they'll be fine. Don't forget he has powers. He will protect Melisa as well as bring her back to the shore for you. Brandon and Greg have to go back and wait; the elders and I will get Melisa and Damien back. Until then, do not do anything crazy—you know what I mean, Viktoria."

"Hush, everybody, I think I can hear Melisa saying something." I looked up at the heavens. "Melisa, can you hear me? If you can, just tell us where you are! Who is next to you?"

"Mom, I can hear you! I am in a cave; it looks like a volcano. There is a burning fire here. I'm scared! They have taken Damien, and I don't know where they took him."

"Did you hear that, Michael?" Brandon said. "I want to come with you and the elders. Lilith might listen to me; do not forget I was on their side before. I know how Lilith and Samuel work; I can do it again."

"No, Brandon, it's too dangerous. They already know you. You have betrayed them; they will not trust you anymore."

"Look, Michael, whatever happened, it was my fault. If I weren't so power-hungry, these things would never have happened. It's entirely my fault; now I must face the consequences. I need to save my children from Lilith, whatever the results are. I'm ready."

"Viktoria," Michael said, looking at me, "tell Brandon that he cannot come with us. I don't want to lose him as well. What if she keeps all three of them? We have Lilith aggravated; there is no telling what she will do. The elders and I will handle Lilith; let us do what we need to do.

"Viktoria, the elders, Alia, and I will be going back. Your father will join us, as well. We have to go back where we did the ceremony. There must be a door that is still open; I don't know how this could have happened, but it did."

The driver took us back to the church; I could not believe my eyes. Parts of the church had been torn down. There were police cars and ambulances everywhere; I called Cameron's and Lacey's names a couple of times before they answered me. For a moment, I thought something had happened.

"Mommy," Cameron called out, "we are over here by the ambulance!"

"Oh, my God, Brandon, something happened to your mom! Why else would they be in the ambulance?"

"Calm down, Viktoria, the EMTs are probably just checking to make sure everyone is okay."

"Cameron, what happened to Grandma Nelly? And where is your sister?"

"Lacey is next to Grandma Nelly, but we have not seen Melisa. She's missing. The police and volunteers are looking for her. Grandma Nelly was not feeling well, so they're checking up on her to see if she's okay and are giving her medicine."

"Brandon, go call off the search. Tell them that Melisa just called; she's at home and is okay. I'm going to Nelly to see if she's okay."

"Excuse me," Brandon said, going up to a policeman, "I would like to talk to someone in charge of the search for Melisa. I'm her father, and I have news regarding her."

"Yes, that's Sergeant Dudukov, over there," the policeman said pointing to the sergeant. "He's in charge of the search. Let me get him for you. Sergeant Dudukov, this gentleman is Melisa's dad; he says he has news about her."

"Hi," the older gentleman said, "I am Sergeant Dudukov."

"I am Melisa's dad; she just called me and said she got scared and had her friend take her home. She's fine; you can call off the search. Please except my apologies for any trouble this has caused you."

"Okay then. Sorry, I did not get your name."

"It's Brandon Nelson."

"Okay, Brandon; I'm glad your daughter is safe. I will call everyone back then. When you get a chance, tell Melisa we would like to see her and thank her for helping us with the casualties."

"I will do that, Sergeant, as soon as she feels up to it. Thank you."

"How is your mother doing?"

"I don't know; my wife is with her. I have not seen her yet; I hope she's okay. There's my wife now; we'll find out. Hi, honey, Sergeant Dudukov was asking how Mom is doing."

"She is just fine. Nelly got a bit excited; you know how her heart is. It just beats faster than normal when she gets excited."

"I know you; aren't you the famous police psychic, Viktoria Nelson? We were talking about you the other day. We have a new captain; she has worked with you before. Her name is Lilith; she said she is a good friend of yours. But she did not mention that Melisa is your daughter."

"Yes, I am Viktoria. As for being famous, I don't know about that. Oh yes, if Lilith is here, I would love to see her."

"Well, she was asking questions; I'm sure she's still here."

"It was nice talking to you, Sergeant. Thanks for your great help; I will stop one day at the station. I'll see you then." I turned to my husband once the sergeant was gone. "Brandon, let's go see what Lilith wants from us. I know if she is here, she wants to talk to us."

"Do you want me to get the holy water, the salt, the gold dagger, and the cross? Aren't you going to call Michael and tell him that Lilith is here?"

"Brandon, if you remember correctly, Michael said don't do any out-of-body experiences. He did not mention that we could not talk to Lilith or make a deal when we see her, right? By the way, none of those will work with Lilith."

"Viktoria, how are we going to tell who Lilith is? I'm sure she will be in disguise."

"Don't worry, Brandon, she will make sure that we do recognize her."

"Look, Viktoria, at the lady behind that guy over there," he said, pointing. "Her eyes are looking straight at us. I think it's her."

"You're right. It's her. Let's go to her." As we moved closer and closer to Lilith, she was taking a step back each time. "Lilith, wait! We need to talk to you!"

"Meet me at the back. I will catch up with you."

"Brandon, keep your eyes open, and do not move away from my side. Have your protection on, not that you need it. After all, she is your buddy."

"Viktoria, I don't find that funny at all. I am sorry that I made that mistake. Believe me, I am paying for it."

"No, Brandon, we are all paying for it. If you hadn't joined that cult, whatever it was, and if you weren't so success-hungry, we would not be going through this right now!"

"Viktoria, we are doing just what she wants us to do. We're turning against each other! She is manipulating us, so she will get what she wants from both of us! Let me talk to her and explain everything to her. She might let them free, or I'll ask her to take me instead. I am the one she's furious with."

"Good plan, Brandon," Lilith said. "Just one thing: I am furious with someone else also! If I wanted to get back at you for how you betrayed me, I would have done it by now! It is you, Viktoria, that I want! I will return Melisa, but you also have to tell the archangels and the elders to back off and leave my demons alone."

"No, Lilith, you have to let both Damien and Melisa go. Then I will come with you; I'll do whatever you want."

"What are you talking about? We have not taken Damien; he is not with us."

"Lilith, you do not even have Melisa!" I said, finally figuring it out. "You're just trying to trick me into coming with you! You thought you could kill two birds with one stone by asking me for information. Okay, Lilith, where are Melisa and Damien? What demon were they with? Who got them? I see you are scared, Lilith! Now, let's talk!" I demanded.

"It is Lucifer," she said. "He has them. He found out about my plans. There is no way of knowing what he will do to them. If you don't believe me, ask Melisa. I know you can talk to her using your telepathy; if you ask me, Lucifer won't hurt Melisa or Damien and all because of you."

"What do you mean because of me? What does this have to do with me?"

"Viktoria, Lucifer fell in love with you at Brandon's hospital's grand opening. He decided to have you, and he was determined, so he asked for my help."

"That was about twenty-one years ago. I don't remember ... I don't even know what he looks like."

"That night, he asked me to keep Brandon away from you, and I did whatever he told me. Well, that night, you thought you were making love to Brandon, but unfortunately, it was Lucifer."

"No!" I yelled, horrified. "It can't be! You're lying! This is not true; that is impossible! You are only saying these things to get back at me!" I looked at my husband. "Brandon, why don't you say something? Tell her that that is not true! How could you just stand there! Tell her it was you! I made love to you that night! You even opened the champagne to celebrate your success!"

"I am sorry, Viktoria. I did not come home that night. I even called and told you that there was a problem in the hospital. I came home the next morning."

"Oh, how can this be true? It can't! Please, God, tell me this is not! Brandon, that was the night Melisa was conceived! He cannot be her father, my baby!"

"If you don't believe me Viktoria, ask Melisa about the little brown scar she has behind her left ear. It looks like a three-leaf clover at first. But if you check it with a magnifying glass, it is 666."

"I still don't believe you, Lilith! You have to take me to Lucifer! I have to talk to him! See if he has something to tell me, something he wants to say face-to-face."

"I will help you, but you have to ask the elders and archangels to give me back my hundreds of demon babies and open the doors to hell that they have closed."

"Lilith, I cannot promise you that. I will see Lucifer with or without your help.

"If I were you, I would make a deal. There is something else—"

"I don't believe anything you say anymore."

"When you see Lucifer, ask him about the other child."

"What child?" Brandon asked.

"Viktoria," Brandon said, holding on to my arm, "you cannot do this. It's not safe; we have to tell the elders that we need their help first."

"No, Brandon, I am going and getting my kids back home, where they belong. If you want, you can call Greg and tell him everything. He'll know how to get in touch with me, but no elders, Brandon. Do you understand? I will let Lacey know when we need the elders' help. Please take Nelly and the kids home."

"I cannot let you go by yourself. I am coming with you; don't try to stop me."

"Brandon, you have to stay with Nelly and the kids. They need you. Just take them home soon. When I get the kids, I will be joining you at home." I touched his cheek with my fingertips. "Don't worry about me. I'll be fine."

"No way; I don't want to send you alone. I will never forgive myself if anything happens to you."

"Brandon, nothing will happen to me; believe me. You know what? If I don't come back in two hours, you can contact the elders and tell them everything."

"I still say I should come with you, Viktoria. I know how Lilith works. How do we know if she is telling us the truth? Did you ever think about that?"

"Yes, I did. Nevertheless, she wants something back, and she will get it only if I get my kids back from Lucifer."

"Hold on a second; if you don't trust me, how can I trust you? How do I know the elders won't follow us over there?" Lilith demanded.

"You don't know, just like I don't know, so we have to deal with whatever happens, don't we, Lilith? So you better take me to Lucifer now."

"As long as you don't mention this to the elders, I will take you to him. Then, if there is nothing else, now you deal with Lucifer. I am not going against Lucifer to get you your kids."

"Don't worry. You have about two hours. Otherwise, Brandon will tell them everything."

"Well, meet me at your place; then we will go as soon as you get home."

"What are you talking about?"

"I just want you to meet me at your house, in the basement. Well, maybe Brandon can explain to you why on the way."

"Brandon, what is she talking about? Our house?"

"I will tell you as soon as we get home, Viktoria. First let's take everyone home."

When we got home, Brandon led me to the extended section of the basement.

"Viktoria, I know you do not like the extended section of the basement, but we have to talk in there if you want to see Lucifer and Lilith."

"Why in there, Brandon? What is it? You know I don't like the dark; I don't feel comfortable here."

"I'm just going to explain everything once when we get inside. Otherwise, you will not understand."

As we went inside, I was surprised to see that it was totally fixed up. I hadn't been in the basement for a long time—since the time I found a goat's head buried in there; it was a terrible experience. Brandon bent down and picked up a pile of wood from the floor.

Then I heard someone coming toward the basement. At first, I got scared, and then I realized it was my mom.

"Viktoria, what are you doing? Why are you opening this door? This is dangerous; you cannot do this by yourself."

Then I heard Michael and Babushka. They were frustrated with Brandon; they yelled at us, screaming, "You will never learn!" and "This is the door the demons have been using!" I was in shock, but I could not say anything, because this was my chance to get my kids back from Lucifer. No one was going to stop me.

"Babushka, you cannot stop me. I have to get the kids! Lilith should be here shortly. Please go away; otherwise, she will not take me to him."

"Who is he, Viktoria? Is that Lucifer? She told you that Melisa was conceived by Lucifer. Now she is taking you to face him and ask for your kids back. What does Lilith want in return? I can tell you right out, but read this. Then make sure to spray holy water on it to dissolve the writing."

"You knew, Babushka. This means you also knew about the other child," I said in shock. "Why does it seem like everyone knew but me? Why didn't you tell me this before? How could you keep this from me, Babushka? Lilith asked me to talk to the elders and the archangels and said that you have to return her babies that they have taken from her. Also, she wants to be ranked higher than Adam, Eve, and Lucifer. She said history does not mention her as Adam's first wife and mother of the demons."

"All right. Go to your reading room and make a circle with crystal salt and gold daggers. Then make a cross. Stand on it and read it. Then spray the holy water; do not come out of the circle until it has all dissolved. This is only for you, not Brandon. I am sorry, Brandon, but you are still under Lilith's influence. It is best if you do not know yet."

As soon as I got the letter, I ran into my reading room and did exactly what Babushka had told me to do. I was right in the middle, standing on the gold daggers, when my mom appeared right next to me. At least I was not alone at this moment.

"I have found out," she said softly, "that Lucifer fathered the twins, not Melisa. The reason Lucifer has taken Melisa is to get Damien and tell him the truth and ask him to stand by him."

"Mom, you knew this too? What about what Lilith told me? And another child, is it true?"

"No, baby, it's not. She just wanted to use you to get her demon babies back and turn Damien against you, believe me. Your dad has tried to tell you so many times, but he could not. Don't be angry with him."

"I don't know, Mom; I am so confused. I don't know what to say. I better go back; Babushka's waiting for me to decide what to do. I don't know what to believe anymore."

"Viktoria, just do what is right for you, and listen to your heart. To determine what is right and what is wrong, just think about your father. Do what he is saying."

"Okay, Mom. I really need to go now. Please stay with the kids until I come back."

I went to the basement. I did not know what to do, what to say. How was I going to tell Brandon the truth?

"Viktoria, did you make up your mind?"

"Yes, Babushka, I did. I am going with Lilith. I have to save my kids. I advise you and Michael to find a way to deal with Lilith."

"We cannot do that. There is no chance that she will get her demon babies, Viktoria. Let us handle everything. You are putting yourself and the kids at risk of never coming back from hell. Back away from this before it is too late."

"I think you and the elders should leave now. I believe Lilith should be here soon, and she especially requested not to have you or the elders around when she gets here. So please leave, Babushka."

He nodded and left. A few minutes later, Lilith walked in. "There you are, Lilith; you made it."

"I would not miss this for anything. I always get what I want, either way. Come on, let's go then. What are you waiting for?"

I went over to Brandon and gave him a hug. "Brandon," I whispered in his ear, "just take care of the family until I come back. Tell Alia to keep an eye on Lacey and Cameron."

He whispered back, "I will tell her. Just be careful; don't trust Lilith. I love you."

"I love you too, honey, no matter what happens."

"Come, Viktoria," Lilith said, grabbing me by the arm. "We are leaving; it's not time to express your feelings to each other. Hold on to me. We are going to jump right in. Don't let go of my shoulder."

We jumped into the hole. Lilith looked very different; she was actually flying right into the fire. I was scared of the flames, and it was getting hotter as we went deeper. I was trying to hold on to Lilith, but suddenly, I slipped away and started falling down.

"Lilith, help me! Lilith, get me out of here! Why won't you answer me?"

"Michael, we have to freeze time! Please! Or else she will fall into the loop and then we cannot save her!"

"Illia, I don't know if we can do that. That is hell, and we don't know where Lilith is. She could use this for a way out."

"Please, Michael. We have to take a chance; we have to save her and the kids."

"All right, but only for a minute. You hold on to me. I will grab and bring her up."

"Look, Michael, it won't even take a minute; just tell me when."

"Illia, now! Go get her! Make sure no other demons are around, including Lilith!"

"Michael, what is going on? It looks like I am moving backward; everything is swirling. Oh no! I see Damien and Lilith!"

"Illia, I think Lilith used Damien to reverse time and go back to save his mother."

"How far is she taking us back, Michael?"

"I am afraid, but I think the night of the twin's birth. That means the rest of the six hundred sixty-five are reborn. I think Lilith did something good for us; this could mean we can turn everything for our advantage."

"What about my wife and me? Will we be alive?"

"No, Illia, you will never be alive again. But you and your wife can make yourselves visible to everyone. I think we are in the hospital now. Look, Viktoria is there and the rest of the family; we shall join them as well."

"Illia, if I know Viktoria, when she wakes up, she'll be questioning us. What could time reversal be used for?"

"We did not reverse the time. It was Lilith. The elders and I froze time to save Viktoria from falling into the loop of fire. Then Lilith took the advantage and used Damien to reverse it."

# Chapter 16

## *In Hell*

"Forget everything and go back to the night of the demon babys' birth. Lilith will be after Damien to get back at Lucifer and the angels who took her babies."

"This means she knows Viktoria's twins are from Lucifer. Plus, Damien has powers from Lucifer and the angels. Lilith knows everything now."

"Don't worry; we have taken a precaution. At the moment, she is in hiding. As soon as she's out, we will gather the female babies and do their exorcism and baptize all."

"The twins? How we are going to tell Viktoria who fathered the twins? What happens if Lilith reveals the truth to Lucifer?"

"I don't think she knows. Besides, Lucifer might find out what her plans were. Lilith would not like Lucifer to find out about the twins, especially Damien. The elders took the twins under protection as soon as they were born."

"What did they do that for? What about the twins?"

"No, dear, they are under the elders' care. They switched the souls of the twins, not the bodies, or else Lilith would know they had been switched."

"How?"

"There are two types of angels that have taken over their bodies. Viktoria and Brandon won't know anything."

"Lucifer will eventually figure it out. We have to do something about it! You have to talk to the elders and Michael. Lilith will find a way to recreate everything and start hurting those babies at the first chance she gets."

"Let me handle that when the time comes. The elders and I will do something by then. We will take it day by day."

\* \* \*

"Viktoria," Brandon said, walking over to where I lay on the bed. "Wake up. Are you okay? Wake up, Viktoria? Are you all right?"

"I want my babies! I need to help them! Lilith has come back! You need to get me out of here and save my kids. Babushka, where are you? I need your help!"

"Viktoria, wake up! Brandon, you better get the doctor and Babushka. Viktoria, you're hallucinating."

"Doctor Justin, what is going on? She's hallucinating; she's saying things that don't make any sense."

"Don't worry, Brandon. She's having hallucinations because of the sedative we've been giving her for the last two days. She should wake up soon. Just don't leave her by herself."

"Of course we won't. We're all here, next to her."

"Mom, where are you?"

"I am here, baby. It was only a dream; everything's okay."

"Oh my God!" I said, sitting up. "Where am I? What is happening?" I turned to my mother. "Mom, where is Lilith? Where is Lacey and Damien and my babies? Are they okay?"

"Viktoria, who is Lilith? Who are Damien and Lacey? You're having a nightmare, honey."

"Mom, where am I?"

"You are in the hospital."

"Why am I in the hospital? Did something happen?"

"Yes, honey, you were in a car accident two days ago. It was a small one, but they had to take the babies because your blood pressure was high and uncontrollable. You went into early labor."

"What are you talking about, Mom? What babies?"

"The twins, honey. Of course you don't remember. Viktoria, you've been sleeping for the past two days. It was a difficult operation; you need to relax."

"Mom, it was a terrible dream! I thought the babies died, and I could not help them!"

"Viktoria, the babies are fine. Nelly and Babushka are next to them, and Brandon will be here soon. When you feel better, they are going to bring the twins to you. Oh, look! Here's Brandon."

"But I thought the boys died. Oh, Brandon, it was terrible!"

"No, honey, they did not die. And it is not two boys; it's a boy and a girl. It's over, Viktoria. You are going to be fine and so are the twins."

"I must have had a nightmare, but everything looked real! How can I see all these dreams in two days! And they had a real effect, like this! I am still under the influence of the dreams. There was a lady named Lilith, and she was Adam's first wife—"

Brandon wrapped an arm around me. "You're trembling, Viktoria. It was only a dream. You are going to be fine; plus, you were under the influence of the drugs. It's normal to have unusual dreams that seem very real."

"They are getting the twins ready to see you. They are so cute, healthy, and ready to meet their mommy!" Mom looked over at the door. "Look, honey! There they are!"

"Oh, my God, they are so small! I don't know how we're going to handle them and what we're going to name them." The nurse took the twins back to the nursery.

I looked up. "Brandon, Nelly is coming." When my mother-in-law walked in, I said, "Brandon and I were just talking about what we were going to name them."

"Oh dear, Viktoria, you must have forgotten. You already named them. Look at their picture frame; you made it yourself."

"Let me see that, Nelly. I remember now; Alia and Damien, just like in my dream. But who is Gabriellele?"

"Actually, there was a nurse holding your hand during the operation, and her name was Gabriellele."

"How is my little girl doing?" Babushka asked as he came into the room. "I see you are doing much better, Viktoria. You gave us a bit of a scare."

"Hi, Babushka. Have seen your grandchildren yet?"

"Yes, I did. I have been here since you had them. They are so adorable, just like angels."

I groaned. "Babushka, please no mention of any angels or devils for the next few days."

"You know what? We better go home so you can get your rest and enjoy your babies. We have been here for the last two days; I think your mom and Nelly need to rest, so when you come home, they both will be able to help you."

"Thanks, Babushka. I do appreciate everyone's support. I will be seeing you all at home tomorrow."

"Viktoria, I am glad you and the twins are okay. When we heard you had been in an accident, I was worried."

"Why, Brandon?"

"I wanted to stay with you, but instead, I went to work."

"I don't remember. The last thing I remember is I went with Lilith to hell to see if I could find Melisa and Damien. Lucifer suddenly appeared. I was holding on to Lilith. I lost my grip and fell into a hell of fire trying to save the kids."

"That does sound horrible, but it was only a dream, honey. Try not to think about it. Get your rest; I will be next to you all night."

"Before I woke up, I thought I heard a conversation about Lucifer fathering our twins and how they were going to tell me."

"I think you really should stop thinking about it," Brandon said when I told him my concerns. "It was only a dream, and it was horrifying because you were under the influence of the medication that they gave you. Also, the dream occurred in twenty-seven years! This is impossible; you are not even twenty-seven yourself!"

"Brandon, I think I agree with you. It must be the medication, and it was a dream. When are they going to bring the babies into our room to stay?"

"I think they'll bring the babies anytime you want. If you like, I will ask the nurse if we could have them stay next to us; what do you say?"

"Do you think we will be able to keep them all night with us?" I asked, not even daring to hope for so much. "Please, go ask Justin if we can."

"He has left already, but I will call him." He grabbed the phone and dialed. "Hi, Justin. Good, good. Listen, Viktoria and I were wondering if we could have the twins in our room for the night."

"You can have the twins as long as Viktoria doesn't overdo it," I heard Justin say through the phone, "and get herself worked up. If the twins need changing, make sure the nurse handles it. It's too soon for Viktoria at this time. I will call in and ask the nurse to bring the twins into the room. Give my love to Viktoria."

"I'll tell her. Thanks, Justin." He hung up and looked at me with a smile. "Viktoria, I know you were so happy to hear that. By the way, don't worry; I will be taking care of the twins. You heard him, right, Viktoria? Don't overdo it. The nurse will be bringing them over shortly."

"Hi, Mr. and Mrs. Nelson," a young nurse said, coming into the room after a quick knock on the door. "We're ready to bathe them, but I thought you might like to join me. If you want to, we can bring them here."

"That's an excellent idea!"

"I am sorry; I didn't get your name."

"Oh, sorry. It's Angel."

"Thank you so much, Angel." I looked at her for a second. "Have we met before? You look familiar."

"No, I don't think so. I have recently moved here from Washington DC. Well, if you'll excuse me now, I will go and get the twins."

"I really think I have seen her before. I don't usually forget familiar faces, especially beautiful women like her."

"Viktoria, I'm going to get a cup of coffee. Is there anything you want?"

"Yes, get a cup of tea for me, please."

A few minutes after he left, the nurse—Angel—came back in. "Here we are. All ready for our bath, if Mommy is ready."

"Yes, I am. I'm a bit nervous, but I think with your help, I will be okay with it."

"You undress one, and I'll get the other. Then we'll get a sponge; we'll start with giving them a sponge bath now, and perhaps tomorrow, we will try the baby bathtub."

"Oh my God! He has a finger mark under his arm. It's some sort of birthmark. Angel, please check Alia's underarm and see if she has any marks too."

"Let me see … Oh yes! She does. It looks like a fingerprint; it's an unusual birthmark."

"Can you also check to see if she has any mark behind her ears?"

"What kind of mark?"

"Any kind of birthmark, but dark in color."

"No, I don't see any."

"Thank God! What a relief!"

"What? Is everything okay?"

"No … I mean, yes. It was only a dream I had. More like a nightmare."

"You should not be worried about the nightmares. It's normal for a woman who just had a baby—and on the medication too—to have dreams that scare the living daylights out of her."

"I don't know. I am still a little bit scared. I think I'm still overreacting, but I just can't stop thinking about it."

"You know what, Viktoria? When I was younger, I used to hear my grandma praying into my ear every time she saw me. I always thought that prayer was a game. If you don't mind, I would like to pray into their ears."

"What is it, Angel?"

"Only two little prayers that make the Angelic Rosary airy."

"Brandon," I said when my husband walked into the room, "Angel is about to pray something into the babies' ears. I suppose it is just to comfort them."

"Invocation of the Nine Choirs: Brilliant Seraphim, I call to thee; circle round, bring love to me. Mighty Cherubim, guard my gate; remove from me sorrow and hate. Thrones stand firm, stable be; keep me steady on land or sea. I call dominions, leadership true. May I be fair in all I do. Circles of protection, powers form. Help me weather any storm. Miraculous Virtues hover near. Element energies I summon here. Principalities bring global reform; bless the world and each babe born. Glorious Archangels, show me the way to bring peace and harmony every day. Guardian Angel, Goddess delights, bestow your guiding light upon my family.

"And Gabriellele's Prayer: Hail Mary, full of grace, God is with you. Blessed is the fruit of your womb, the Consort and Son. Holy Goddess, Mother of Earth, work your mysteries for your children, now in the hours of our need. Therefore, mote it be.

"Those two are my favorites," she said. "I really like them."

"They were beautiful; I am touched. Thank you so much. I will pray them in their ears when I get the chance. Will you write them down for me, so I can read this to my family? I already feel so relaxed. Don't you think so, Brandon?"

"Yes, I do. Thank you."

"Sure, Viktoria, it will be my pleasure, but don't forget that it does work every time. Would you like me to leave the twins with you?"

"Yes, please. They are already sleeping; we will be just fine."

"Well, they should be up for milk in a few hours. Please come to the nurses' station, so I can give you the milk for feeding."

"Thank you, Angel. You are a real angel."

"Thanks."

Another nurse came into the room. "Excuse me, Angel? There is a phone call for you."

"Okay, Lillian, wait for me; I am coming."

"Hello, Nurse Angel speaking," she said.

I could hear the voice on the other end.

"Hi, Gabriellele, it's me. How is everything? I believe Michael and the elders already told you what we need you to do."

"Yes, don't be concerned; it is done. Everything went as it should have. Nothing happened, except that she said she recognizes me."

"Try not to stay around her too long. Also change your voice; Viktoria is really good with voices. She could tell who was who even if she were blindfolded. If there is anything unusual or if you have any suspicions, just let me know. Just before you leave, Leila should be there to make sure Viktoria and Brandon keep an eye on the twins. They will be taken care of by Leila."

"How long are we going to have to keep this up?"

"Until we find Lilith and the time goes back."

"What do you mean? I thought you and the elders did it? Reversed time, I mean."

"No, the elders and I froze time for one minute to prevent Viktoria from falling into the demons' loop of fire. Unfortunately, Lilith used that against us and took the time back. In one way, it is to our advantage, but in another, we have to wait for Damien. When he turns six, he'll understand his powers. Also, we have to wait for Lilith to return."

"What if you cannot find her?"